LAURA LOST HER SMILE

Jarlon Magee

PublishAmerica
Baltimore

© 2012 by Jarlon Mageev.
All rights reserved. No part of this book may be reproduced, stored in a retrieval system or transmitted in any form or by any means without the prior written permission of the publishers, except by a reviewer who may quote brief passages in a review to be printed in a newspaper, magazine or journal.

First printing

All characters in this book are fictitious, and any resemblance to real persons, living or dead, is coincidental.

PublishAmerica has allowed this work to remain exactly as the author intended, verbatim, without editorial input.

Softcover 9781462695980
PUBLISHED BY PUBLISHAMERICA, LLLP
www.publishamerica.com
Baltimore

Printed in the United States of America

ACKNOWLEDGMENTS

I want to mention works that were helpful in writing this novel. THE TEMPLE OF GOLD, by William Goldman, novelist and screenwriter extraordinaire; Rudyard Kipling's classic poem, GUNGA DIN; 1950 major motion picture, YOUNG MAN WITH A HORN; FRENCH film classic, A MAN AND A WOMAN (UN HOMME ET UNE FEMME) GRAND PRIZE WINNER, 1966 CANNES FILM FESTIVAL.

I would be remiss if I did not acknowledge the wonderful Film Documentary, STOLEN, directed by Rebecca Dreyfus, based on the still un-solved theft, in 1990, of precious masterpiece art works from the Isabella Stewart Gardner Museum, Boston...

FOR
Joanie...she knows why
IN REMBRANCE OF
Lady

CHAPTER 1

It's three in the morning—the end of December. The sweet whisper of a cornet floats on an easy ride, encapsulating the thinning crowd of jazz lovers still seated around the tables of Brooklyn's Blue Moon Bar & Lounge. The patrons are transfixed by the cornet player's crystalline notes—so soft and pure they could be the sound of a girl saying 'yes.'

The horn player, Dax Bolton, played his Courtois Cornet as if he was born to play nothing else. Dax suddenly stopped playing as his eyes focused on a young woman making her way out of the New York cold into the warmth of the Blue Moon. Dax saw, and felt, a pale-blue, misty light sweep down and caress this beautiful creature. The jazz patrons wondered why the band leader was suddenly ignoring them, in favor of this intruder who had appeared out of nowhere.

Dax felt that the woman's face was bathed in a near-angelic glow. The woman was cold, and the beauty tugged her trench coat close around her shoulders. She shot a glance at Dax as she rushed to a table near the band-stand.

Dax called a brief intermission and waved the rest of the musicians off the band-stand. His gaze was fixed firmly upon this beauty as he bounded off the stage, and raced to her table.

He felt that time stood still—it was as if he had entered a tragic calm, something referred to by academics as 'the third realm.' Dax felt a blinding white light permeate his being.

He thought back to yesterday morning when he first met this lovely German lady seated before him—his mind replayed their meeting as he recalled every word of their conversation at the Greenwich Village STARBUCKS, and it went something like this:

(THE PREVIOUS MORNING)

"Uh, miss, haven't we met somewhere before—
"I don't think so—is that the best you can do? I bet you say that to all the girls..."
Dax turned reddish-purple, his embarrassment obvious to anyone who happened by. Finally, he managed a grin as he muttered, "Yeah, that was pretty lame. I've been working all night—guess I'm a little worse for the wear and tear..."
"Well, you <u>do</u> look strung-out. You on some heavy-duty drugs?"
"Nah, nothing like that. Just a little too much scotch—the life of a horn player, I suppose..."
"What do you play?"
"Cornet. You a jazz fan?"
"Before we discuss my likes and dislikes, wouldn't an introduction be in order?"
"Of course. Name's Dax. Dax Bolton. And, you're—
"Laura."
"Laura, pleased to meet you," Dax said, his voice broke as his grin metamorphosed into an ebullient smile. "Can we start over—or at least make an attempt?"

"You got it, Dax—sounds like a great idea," replied Laura, a grin beginning to make its way across her porcelain face.

"Well, mister Jazzman, now that we're safely on the road to conversation, what can you tell me about yourself? I can't promise I'll return the favor—you'll have to take your chances—okay?"

"Deal. I've already told you I play cornet—been in love with the cornet since I turned fourteen, back in St. Louis. Not a bad town, but I couldn't wait to get to the Big Apple. Been here since the world entered the 21st century, arriving on New Year's Day, 2001. I'm playing at a club in Brooklyn—the Blue Moon—heard of it?"

Laura smiled at Dax and replied, "Can't say I have...got an address?"

"Well, it's quite a few blocks from where we sit. Corner of 44th & Orange. The Blue Moon caters to hardcore jazz afficandos—one of the only clubs in the city that offers the type of jazz my guys play—"

"And that would be—"

"Cool, breezy, jazz. The kind found primarily in southern California—also known as the West Coast Sound..."

"Oh, yes, although I don't think I've ever heard it played live..."

"Well, now you'll have the opportunity—we play three nights a week—Wednesday, Friday and Saturday nights. And, guess what? Today's Saturday, so we're on this evening—we start a little late for some folk's taste, but that's the way it is..."

"Which is...?"

"Eleven p.m. But, the good news is that sometimes we play 'til three or four in the morning, depending on the mood of the owner.

In fact, we played 'til almost daylight this morning. I haven't been back to my apartment since we turned the

lights out. I'm going to get some rest before we crank it up tonight. Say, why don't you stop by—give us a listen?"
"You didn't tell me the name of your combo—
"Actually, it's a quintet—we're called 'In a Mist'."
"Catchy. 'In a Mist' plays the Blue Moon—sounds rather melancholy..."
"You could say that. Will I see you tonight?"
"A girl can't promise, just like that. However, I would like to hear your quintet—tell you what, if I can manage it, I'll be by sometime late tonight—time doesn't appear to be a problem for you..."

Dax laughed and said, "Well, sometimes I don't get enough rest, that's for sure, but, hell, it's the music—that's my lifeline and it keeps me alive..."

"Listen, Dax, I'm glad we had this conversation—I do look forward to hearing you play live at the Blue Moon, but I've got to be going just now."

Dax reached into his chinos and pulled out a dog-eared business card and handed it to Laura. She glanced at it, smiled briefly, then stuffed it into her Coach purse as she rose to her feet and headed for the exit.

"Wait a sec! You didn't tell me anything about yourself—I don't even know your phone number, nothing..."

She laughed and said, "You'll get it tonight—if I show—okay?"

"Whatever you say," replied Dax.

Laura waved good-bye to Dax as she stepped outside STARBUCKS and briskly paced down the street. Seconds later she disappeared into a subway entrance.

Dax shook his head to clear his thoughts and he was suddenly back in the moment—he realized that he was staring woodenly at Laura, and noted that yesterday's smile had disappeared, and the look on her face struck Dax as an 'archaic smile,' better known as a 'Mona Lisa Smile.' That is, a smile that doesn't seem quite real.

"Laura, this is a wonderful surprise! Really glad you decided to come tonight. By the way, you look wonderful, if I may say so," Dax said, his voice almost a whisper.

"Glad to be here, Dax. Thought I'd take you up on the invite to give the place a once-over. Looks like it has possibilities. What's the name of the number you were playing when I walked in?"

"In a Mist.' That's not only the name of the song but, as you know, the name of my quintet. By the way, 'In a Mist' is the name of a very famous jazz piece by Bix Biderbecke, perhaps the greatest cornetist of all-time—at least in my book, he's the top banana of them all."

Laura studied Dax as he spoke. She noted the serious tone of his voice as he spoke of this Bix Biderbecke. "So, Dax, what can you tell me about this 'cat' you call Bix?"

"Ever heard of the book and movie, YOUNG MAN WITH A HORN?"

Laura smiled and answered that she had not only heard of it, she had seen the movie in an art-house in Berlin, years ago, when she was about twenty years old.

Dax said, "Well, the movie came out in the 50s—Kirk Douglas played the lead—a really tragic story—Bix died at the tender age of twenty-eight—when his life should have been just starting...he was truly unbelievable. I have several of his recordings, but, of course, that's not the same as listening to Bix in person—"

"How did he manage to die so young?"

"Well, it was attributed to a bout of pneumonia, but the fact is, he drank himself to death—he never had time for anything but the music and the booze—that was it. All the rest was just window-dressing, eye-candy, so to speak—extraneous, you might say…"

"Well, no matter how talented he was, he must have needed something more, don't you think?"

"The horn was it—maybe it was enough—maybe it wasn't. Who knows? Like the cliché says, he burned bright and hot, and burned out too early. But, the music—it will live forever," Dax whispered.

"I'm sorry, Laura. I shouldn't have dropped all that on you—

"No problem—please hand me a menu and get your butt back up on that stage and let me hear that horn—I need to see whether you have the chops to compare with Bix or Chet Baker, or whomever else you are chasing…"

Dax smiled at this German beauty and responded, "Okay, you're the boss tonight. Enjoy your dinner while we serenade you with some cool jazz!"

Binx jumped back onto the revolving platform known as the 'Rotunda,' and fitted his favorite mouthpiece into his silver Cornet as he prepared to show Laura what he could do with his horn. He lit into a lesser-known Bix tune—a melancholy, yet peppy number. Silvery notes pealed from the bell of Dax's cornet, the sound flaring over the patrons of the Blue Moon. His tone was so true, so perfectly pitched, that the horn's flight-of-fancy raised goose-bumps on the devoted jazz fans who, for the most part, were regulars at the Blue Moon. Dax heard a patron comment to his date that, "Dax's horn sounded like an aura from above, playing off the corner of the ear-drum, and then seeming to dart away, just as the listener begins to channel into the sound... the chords sliver-thin, the music could be a mist of light from the Garden of Eden, or The Far Pavillions..."

As Dax played, he thought back to a comment he'd heard from one of his regulars..."Dax, your sound conjures up a vision of a doomed bird of gorgeous plumage spreading its wings in a dazzle of sunlight." In his mind's eye, Dax thought back to his boyhood in St Louis...Dax and his fellow school band-mates were high-stepping down a broad road in a jazzy funeral parade—a sight more familiar in the city of New Orleans, the birthplace of Jazz. In true New Orleans fashion, the music was somber on the way to the cemetery; yet jubilant, and sassy, on the trip back...

As Dax finished his cornet solo, he broke loose of his reverie and looked into the eyes of his beautiful visitor. He noted that her blonde hair shone as the light reflected off her face, off her being, with a quiver. He thought that the light surrounding Laura was magical, that the light was alive and capable of stepping into the most euphoric waltz ever conceived...

It occurred to Dax that Laura's aura was reminiscent of the particular Southern California light that he had loved when he had lived and worked in San Diego, many years earlier.

CHAPTER 2

Laura found herself thinking about that strange horn player she'd just met—Dax Bolton. A jazz musician, no less...the irony didn't escape her. After all the miles she'd covered, all the time she'd spent vainly trying to distance her private life—most of all, her love life—from the world of the arts—musicians, actors, dancers, painters, all of them. The life that had consumed most of her early yea rs—twenty-something years of dance—first in Berlin, then several years in Paris; finally, studying and working in Vienna with one of the world masters of modern dance. She knew the danger of being one of those 'lost souls' who dreamed only of performing, of living a life divorced from the 'real world,' those who fancied themselves as 'different' from the rest of humanity.

And, she had come so far for beauty. How far is far enough, she wondered...Laura had trained for the dance with a near-manic devotion and commitment to the discipline. And it had rewarded her—in the beginning. At least she felt that, in a limited way, it <u>had</u> rewarded her—not monetarily, but her reward lay in the satisfaction that she derived from the performance—to perform in front of a live, appreciative audience—that was the ultimate—that was everything to Laura. And, she had, with one glaring exception, avoided the complications of a love-life; she knew that a lover magnified the difficulties of becoming a world-class dancer.

Then again, she really had no choice—her destiny had been charted for her by her father, Victor Vallinsky. Ole Vic, as he was known by friends and family, had been her sole family. Her mom, Beatrice, had died in child-birth, giving life to Laura. And, Laura had carried this burden of guilt with her—every day of her thirty-five years of existence.

Laura and Victor relocated to Berlin after the agonizing death of Laura's mother. Her dad identified with the German people with a tenacity that was hard to understand. It was as if he had felt that he was born out of place, and was more comfortable, more 'himself,' in Deutschland—he had almost succeeding in naming his baby girl Lili Marleen, after the famous WWII song of that name—a favorite of both Germany and the Allies. She had not known the 'real' reason her dad had left Budapest so many years before she was born. She knew that it had something to do with his work, but his work was something he never talked about…

She did know that her mother was also born in Budapest, Hungary, to a second-generation family of gypsys who roamed Eastern Europe ceaselessly, and had done so for the past two centuries. Her mother had been a beautiful woman, slim build with a wonderful mane of jet-black hair which spilled about her pear-shaped face. Victor had, at times, told Laura that her mother's hair-do served to frame her face as if with a mysterious shroud…

Laura had the good fortune to be blessed with her mother's acquiline nose, and large, oval blue-green eyes that appeared to not so much as stare at you, as to look into the very soul of whomever she was speaking to…this was a family trait which turned off some folks…in any event, it was a trait that had been passed on to Laura…

Laura hoped that their meeting at the Blue Moon would be a stepping-stone to a meaningful romance. Already she was fearful of losing him, of letting go, or being let go—at the same time, for reasons that she had not yet revealed to Dax, she was afraid to get too close, because she knew she was in a difficult situation with her dad...Laura didn't know all the details, but she knew that it was a matter of life or death. And, it was likely that her dad would not survive to see her again. He had run afoul of the 'Russian Mafia,' and that was not a good thing. She knew that the problem was not of his making, but circumstances had made him a prime candidate for blackmail.

There were no living relatives in Europe from whom she could ask for help. Laura had moved to New York only months earlier—it was the one request that her dad had made to her due to his fear of the Russian mafia. Her dad had told her that she would soon be contacted by a 'Boris Utterch.' What this Boris would ask her to do, she didn't know. However, the Russian mafia had arranged for Laura to be performing in an off-Broadway show—the gangsters had legitimate contacts throughout the U.S.—as well as both savory and unsavory contacts worldwide.

Whatever was coming, Laura knew she had to wear a mask, a brilliant disguise, to the world-at-large. Laura must meet the world head-on, with all the talent and energy she could muster. She knew she'd do whatever it took to keep her father alive. Did Laura and Dax have a shot at making their romance work? She didn't know—she only knew that she was going to give it her best shot.

CHAPTER 3

Dax didn't know what hit him last night—was it the performance he put on for Laura, or was it just the euphoria of being <u>with</u> that magnificent woman? Whatever it was, it hit him like nothing else he'd experienced in the longest time. Dax had only known Laura for barely twenty-four hours, and yet, although he still knew next-to-nothing about her, the cornet player was as revved up as a seventeen-year-old high-schooler at his senior prom. After the Blue Moon Bar & Lounge closed at four a.m., Dax and Laura decided to have a cup of coffee at Java Dave's in nearby Manhattan. It was in this conversation that Dax learned Laura's full name—Laura Vallinsky, which she had stubbornly kept from him most of the evening. She told Dax that her father had wanted to name her 'Lili Marleen,'—the famous World War II marching song. This tune became a huge international hit—it was written by a German and sung by the famous singer, Lale Andersen. The song was originally embraced by the Germans, then finally adopted and loved by almost everyone. The Brits, Americans, Canadians, even the French—all loved the song. 'Lili Marleen' was most famously recorded by the singer and actress Marlene Dietrich, a native German who had defected from Nazi Germany at the beginning of WWII. Her version was a solid hit in America, as well as the other Allied countries fighting the Nazi war machine. Hitler and Goebbels did not like the song because of their bitterness at Marlene Dietrich for rejecting the Nazi cause.

Laura had confided to Dax earlier that her dad was in serious trouble in Europe, but she wouldn't give him any details. She promised that she would share more information as time went by. For now, Dax was happy at having the good fortune to know this beauty, and planned to get to know her much better. The horn player was not so sure about this thing called 'love at first sight,' but, he thought, if this isn't it, it's awfully close...

CHAPTER 4

Laura stepped onto the train platform in Grand Central Station—she was in a hurry. She knew that the men of DAV-D were waiting for her in Trenton, New Jersey. Laura had decided to go to them, rather than wait for these gangsters to surprise her, unannounced, in the middle of the night, in her apartment, or elsewhere, in New York City. Vic had earlier given the name and cell number of Mikael Pratt to Laura—Pratt was the leader of the DAV-D 'associates' in the Eastern part of the U.S.A. DAV-D is an acronym for a splinter group within what is loosely called the 'Russian Mafia.' DAV-D didn't exist, in an organized fashion, until the collapse of the former USSR. However, once the craziness began, it was reminiscent of the Wild West in frontier America. Shoot-outs were not uncommon—even in the midst of Moscow and other metropolitan areas of Russia. Seems a gangster is a gangster, no matter the geography, no matter the nationality...

The men and women of DAV-D were professional guns-for-hire—modern-day assassins. And Laura knew that her name was near the top of their list. The only reason her name wasn't number one on the hit-list was because of her father. As long as he was alive, she was reasonably 'safe.' The vermin who were part of DAV-D needed her father alive—dead, he was of no further use to them, and, if he was of no further use to them, they had no need to keep Laura alive. They couldn't take the chance that she wouldn't talk to Interpol and reveal secrets that would be devastating to DAV-D.

DAV-D specialized in black-market goods and services. At the top of the nefarious list was international art theft—thugs who care for nothing but the profit they realize from the sale of this precious cargo. Laura's dad had tried, almost one year ago, to alert authorities to DAV-D—he was caught before he could make contact and has been held under 'house arrest' since that time.

The only reason that he was still alive, and the only reason that Laura was still alive, was because they needed her dad—for what reason, Laura didn't know, but she knew that it was the only thing keeping her dad alive—she hadn't dealt with her fears that DAV-D would be coming after her as well, although she knew that was always a possibility...

In less than an hour she stepped off the train at the Trenton, New Jersey station. Just as she feared, three men were anxiously awaiting her arrival. Three men who had one thing in common—they were the 'elite guard' of DAV-D. Laura had never met any of these men, yet she knew instinctively who they were the second she made eye-contact with each of the three men huddled together. They glared at the departing passengers with greedy eyes. She knew, without being told, that the third man to her left, staring at Laura with a savage sneer planted on his ugly face, was none other than Mikael Pratt.

"Halo, Miss Vallinsky. You are Laura Vallinsky, aren't you?" asked Mikael Pratt.

"Yes, I'm Laura Vallinsky. And, you must be Mikael," Laura replied, a trace of mockery in her voice. She struggled to contain the feeling of panic suddenly surging through her body.

"Of course. I am Mikael—we've been waiting a long time to make your acquaintance," replied Mikael as he turned to face his two companions. "Please, let me introduce you to my comrades, Peter Ussery to your right, and Theo Andersson to your left." Ussery and Andersson both took long, exaggerated bows in front of Laura. There were no smiles from either of the two henchmen of Mikael Pratt. It appeared to Laura that this meeting had been rehearsed by Mikael and the two goons were playing their roles as dictated by the leader, Mikael Pratt. Both Ussery and Andersson held stoic, almost non-descript neutral expressions on their faces. Each of their faces may as well be interchangeable masks, Laura thought to herself.

"It's good that you followed our instructions, Laura. And, most importantly, it's <u>very</u> good for your father's health and well-being," Mikael Pratt remarked, his voice a smug growl.

"How is my dad?" Laura's voice rose an octave—the sharpness of her tone caught the three gangsters by surprise.

"He's good—as good as anyone could be, considering his 'situation,' if you will…"

"Where are we going?" Laura asked, her voice almost inaudible as she fought back the tears burning her eyes.

"You'll know soon enough—don't worry your pretty little head about that," Mikael whispered in Laura's ear as his two goons hailed a taxi. In a matter of seconds, the foursome were speeding into downtown Trenton, New Jersey.

CHAPTER 5

Dax arrived at the Blue Moon much earlier than his usual time, which normally was an hour before the other musicians usually showed up for work. He was glad he had remembered to fetch his favorite mouth piece from the silver-smith who had promised Dax that his mouthpiece would be pristine before show-time. Dax gripped tightly onto the handle of the carrying case housing his beloved Courtois Cornet. The Courtois factory in Paris, France, is the oldest brass instrument-maker in the world. It is an institution known to serious horn players and collectors world-wide, located on Rue de nancy, Paris. The Courtois workers still hand-hammer the bells of the cornets. The owners moved into their current location in 1860 and are still there today. Courtois has manufactured top-quality musical brass instruments since the late 1700s, and Courtois is reputed to have made musical instruments for Napoleon. Dax acquired his Courtois Cornet by accident. He had covered a gig for a pal—a cornetist named Buddy Haloran, a Chicago native. Haloran was on the run from some very angry loan sharks from the Windy City, and Buddy had to make a hasty getaway from New York—so quickly that he sold his Courtois Cornet to Dax in exchange for the money that Buddy owed the sharks. Buddy had known better than to risk his life over the horn—even a grand Courtois Cornet. But, a beautiful instrument like the Courtois Cornet needed a mouthpiece as magnificent as the instrument itself, so when Dax accidentally dropped it on the mean sidewalks of Brooklyn, he had turned to his most trusted silver-smith, located in the Bronx. The thing about the cornet—its raison d'etre (reason for being) was the tone...the tone is what most differentiates the cornet from the trumpet—the tone, due to the configuration of the bell, is concave, whereas the bell of the trumpet is straight. And the hand-made bells of the Courtois Cornet are considered to be among the best in the universe.

Dax was worried—he hadn't heard anything from Laura for two days. The last thing she had told him was that she would be taking a day-trip to Trenton, New Jersey, concerning a matter on which she wouldn't elaborate—other than to tell Dax that it had something to do with her dad, and that was all she had to say on the subject. Laura should have been back sometime yesterday, but she hadn't returned his cell-phone calls and she hadn't returned to New York.

He had already decided that if she didn't show at the Blue Moon, as she had promised, then he would have to do <u>something</u>—the problem was that he didn't have a clue what that something would be...

CHAPTER 6

It had been over one week since Dax had heard from Laura. She was supposed to be gone only two days and then back in New York on the noon train at Grand Central Station. Well, even though there had been no word from Laura, Dax made the trip to Grand Central to meet the noon train. It was no use—she never showed. Dax had waited on the next two arrivals from Trenton, the first at 3:30 pm, and the last one at nine pm...Same result—no Laura.

Dax had wanted to alert the NYPD about Laura's disappearance, but she had assured him that if she were delayed, she'd let him know when she would return—well, that hadn't worked—he'd heard nothing since the morning she left for Trenton.

Dax did the only thing he could think to do—what he always did when things got too crazy and he couldn't think straight—cuddle up to a Johnnie Walker Black neat scotch. He had scheduled a practice session for his combo, In a Mist, for two pm today—but he knew now that he was going to cancel the session. He couldn't concentrate on the music when he was worried sick about Laura—hell, he'd only met her a few weeks ago, and in that short time already knew he was crazy in love with her...

There was no way in hell he was going to be able to do nothing—he <u>had t</u>o do <u>something</u>...but, what the hell would it be?

He decided he'd find a place where no one knew him, a place where he could drink all night if he wanted, a place where he could blend into the nothingness...

And, that portal to nothingness was a club called The Shades, located just off the borough of Manhattan in the Bronx, not far from Yankee Stadium. It was an accident that Dax found the place at all. He was already dizzy from the scotch he'd downed at the Blue Moon when he went to let the boss know that In a Mist would not be playing that evening. In the darkness of a dreary New York City night he missed the entrance to The Shades—he veered into an alley, came out on a narrow street—a street of no return. Maybe this is it, thought Dax. Maybe this is the street of my dreams. No, Lady Luck is a hell of a lot more fickle than that. Dax began to run—at the end of the block he turned left, peered through the dark, looked for a familiar landmark. Finally, he saw an orange glow—his head throbbed from too much scotch, his throat was on fire, his wind-blasted lungs hurt. Worst of all, his legs were heavy and getting heavier, his knees giving way. Made no difference, he staggered on, closer, to that oasis in the night called The Shades.

Dax opened the door and walked into the bar. A lone juke-box wailed the blues. A photo of Texas Bluesman Lightning Hopkins hung high above the juke-box. The place was packed—not a single chair or bar-stool was unoccupied. Dax wasn't looking for a chair. He wasn't looking for anyone—he was in need of another shot of scotch. A view-blurring fog of tobacco smoke conjured up a ghostly sheen over the customers at bar. Everyone in the bar seemed to Dax as if they were opaque—he felt as if he were in a dream. Or maybe I'm the dream, thought Dax—maybe I'll never see Laura again...

No one noticed Dax as he almost tripped over a case of Bud Light lying beneath the bar. What kept him on his feet was the sight of the woman. She sat at the end of the bar on a circular stool, slightly bent over a drink, aiming a dim and faraway smile at nobody. She was dressed completely in white, a sheer fabric clung to her like life itself. A drop-dead beautiful blonde. The kind that, as Raymond Chandler's iconic fictional private eye, Philip Marlowe, once remarked," would make a priest kick a hole in a stained glass window." Her hair was a honey-blonde mane that spilled over her shoulders. Eyes like blue diamonds, soft, moist lips, and a satin-smooth skin which normally would have conspired to make Dax want to grab her and hold her tight against him, as if to fend off all comers. But, that was before he met, and fell instantly in love with the mysterious Laura, the German vanished lady.

But this was no stranger—this was someone whom he had seen with Laura just one week ago. The woman slowly focused on Dax, took in his soft grey eyes, the bewildered look on his face, and his seemingly distraught manner, and noted his wrinkled, patched jacket and chinos.

"Remember me?" Dax asked the woman, his face a mask of desperation.

"Should I?"

"One week ago—you were with Laura—Laura Vallinsky..."

"Yes, I was with Laura a few days ago—what's that got to do with you?"

"I'm Dax—Dax Bolton—I play cornet—at the Blue Moon..."

"So, what else is new? And, what's that got to do with me? By the way, my name is Greta—maybe Laura's mentioned me?"

"Do you know where Laura is? She made a trip to Trenton, New Jersey, and was supposed to be back in New York hours ago—I haven't heard a word from her since she left—"

"No, I don't know anything about that—I do remember that she told me she had to leave town for a day or two—didn't say why..."

"Greta, pleased to meet you. Listen, anything you can tell me is appreciated—I'm really worried about her—all I know is that this meeting had something to do with her dad—who seems to be in some sort of trouble in Russia...

"I don't know anything about that—Laura and I work together—she did tell you that she's doing an off-Broadway show..."

"Yes, of course—I should have put that together—she has mentioned you a time or two—when I saw the two of you together, I didn't approach either of you because I didn't want to interrupt—or make Laura think I was following her—"

"Were you—following her?"

"Well, not exactly—but I am worried about her—this business her father is mixed-up in—do you think she is somehow involved in any of that?"

"I don't have a clue. Tell you what, Dax. If you do hear from her, please let me know, and I'll do the same should I hear anything—okay?"

"You got it—if I don't hear something soon, I'm going to have to go to the police with a missing persons report."

"You might not want to do that just now..."

"Why do you say that? You holding something back on me?"

"No. Not at all—it's just that, if her dad is mixed up in something serious—you just referred to the 'Russian Mafia.'

If that's the case, anything is possible," Greta said, a trace of irony in her voice. "Dax, here's my business card. Say, is this love affair something serious? Laura has mentioned to me that she's mad about you—oops, I shouldn't have said that..."

"Yes, it's for real—that's one reason I'm going crazy with worry—of course, I'd be worried about her safety in any event, but I've never fallen so hard, so fast, for anyone before...," Dax's voice began to falter.

"Here's my cell phone, Greta. Let's keep in touch—okay?"

"You got it—nice to meet you, Dax. Looks like you might call it a night and get some rest—what do you say?"

"I think you're right—this scotch has done all it can do to calm me for the moment. Thanks for sharing the info with me, and let's hope for the best for Laura's return."

"Good night, Dax. I'm calling it a night as well." Greta replied as she slid off her bar-stool and headed for the door.

CHAPTER 7

Laura felt as if her wrists were bleeding—the slightest movement of either hand only brought excruciating pain. She finally managed a peek at the only light she could see from her perch over-looking a circular stairway—an ancient clock which chimed every hour on the hour. Two a.m. Laura had lost count of the number of days she had been imprisoned in her perch. She guessed that it had been almost one week since her meeting with Mikael and his associate. And, in that week she had been subjected to an intense interrogation/torture routine—well, it was anything 'but' routine, and it had taken a toll on her—physically and mentally.

Mikael and his partner wanted more information than she was able to give. Actually, she had told them everything she knew, but they didn't believe her. Mikael and his associates believed that she knew everything her dad had been involved in and could name places, dates, etc...the fact of the matter was that Laura had NOT been privy to the score, so to speak, because her father had anticipated, years earlier, that dire circumstances could arise, therefore, the 'less Laura knew,' the safer she would be...

The problem with that plan was that Mikael had become convinced that Laura was toying with them and she was withholding info. He was now furious with her, and he was poised to take extreme measures—that is, disposing of Laura—like a piece of rubbish. Mikael and his 'friends' knew only too well that certain 'occasions' demanded the 'final solution,' and they were eagerly willing to do whatever it took to stay out of the long eye of the law, whether that law be Scotland Yard, the French secret service, Interpol, the FBI and/or CIA, you name it—they knew to stay out of the cross-hairs—that was the way it was, and that was the way it would always be...

CHAPTER 8

(SIX MONTHS EARLIER)

VIENNA, AUSTRIA—STATE POLICE (SECRET SERVICE HEADQUARTERS)

"OK, Vallinsky, let's go over this one more time. Until we get it straight. You say you're not working for the FSB—the successor to Russia's infamous KGB—is that correct?" asked Friedrich Fellner, Chief Inspector of Austria's Secret Service.

Victor Vallinsky was tired—not just tired, wasted. He had been kept awake for the past thirty-six hours, with only a few minutes of sleep, and his nerves were worn thin. He stifled a yawn, stretched his aching muscles and looked Inspector Fellner in the eye. "For the record, yes, that is correct—I am NOT working for the FSB. I am not working for <u>any</u> Russian agency. What I have been trying to tell you, for the past two days, is that I have been forced by the Russian mafia to '<u>assist</u>' them in a number of heists that have taken place in the art museums of Vienna, Berlin, and Paris. These are dangerous characters—they have forced me to play ball with them…if I don't, at least, 'pretend' to go along with them, they have threatened to harm my daughter, living in New York City. Her name, as I've already told your associates, is Laura. Laura Vallinsky. She is a trained dancer—studied in Berlin and Paris since she was nine years of age—she will soon be working in an off-Broadway musical theater that will open in a few months in New York."

Inspector Fellner adjusted his glasses, glared at his prisoner, and then grabbed his cell phone and punched in a number. "Johan, come here—I need to talk to you—now!"

In seconds, Johan Slottman waltzed through the door and stopped in front of Inspector Fellner. "What can I do for you, sir?"

Fellner, never taking his eyes off his prisoner, asked "kindly read aloud your report, word for word, to Mr. Vallinsky."

Slottman cleared his throat, shot a worried glance at Inspector Fellener, then began reading, his voice a dull monotone:

FROM: RG (GENERAL INTELLIGENCE DIRECTORATE) PARIS, FRANCE
ATTENTION: CHIEF INSPECTOR: STATE POLICE—VIENNA, AUSTRIA

This message is sent with the highest priority—for your eyes only:

Slottman cleared his throat and looked, once again, in the Inspector's direction, then paused, as if waiting for permission to continue..."Well, Slottman, get on with it—READ IT!"

"Yessir—right away, sir! Here's the message...We have information of a most grave and urgent matter which needs your immediate attention and handling. It concerns an agent of the FSB, named Victor Vallinsky, code name: ALGONQUIN. Here's his bio as far as we can ascertain:

Laura Lost Her Smile   31

Born in Budapest, Hungary, on November 2, 1939, parents were Alfred and Irina Jacobson, natives of Budapest, Hungary. They have only the one daughter, Laura, born in 1979. Currently working in New York City, USA. Trained in classical ballet in Berlin and Paris. Victor Vallinsky's parents were Hungarian gypsys...wandering nomads. His mother and father traveled all over Eastern Europe in the early years of the twentieth century, finally settling in Vienna.

Inspector Fellner shouted, "Stop!" He motioned for Slottman to be seated and walked over to the prisoner, stopped directly in front of Victor Vallinsky and silently stood there—staring a hole into the prisoner's eyes. "Well, Victor, do you have anything to add to this report? Any errors we need to clear up before we proceed?"

Victor wearily shook his head 'no' and motioned for Fellner to go on with the reading. Slottman looked to the Inspector for direction, and getting none, sat in stony silence. Finally, tired of the waiting game, Inspector Fellner spoke up. "Finish the report, Slottman—let's see what the prisoner has to say when you get to the bottom line..."

"Yes Sir!" responded Slottman as he abruptly stood up, adjusted his reading glasses, and began reading, his voice so loud it was almost a shout: "Of course, Sir, here's the rest of the text: "After settling in Vienna, at the end of the nineteenth century and the beginning of the twentieth century, a period known as 'fin-de-siecle' in Vienna—a French phrase, referring to the world-weary mood of European Culture, beginning in the 1880s and 1890s, when writers and artists adopted an 'art for art's sake' attitude which was reflected in everything from architecture to artwork, literature, et al—it was a reaction against naturalism and realism—they sought a pure beauty removed from the dreary imperfections of nature and from the drabness of contemporary society. Also, it meant the 'end of an era,' and the beginning of a new era, with a feeling of hope for a fresh start in the new century.

The French also have a term for the turn of the century: 'Belle Epoque' which means 'Beautiful Era.' A 'Golden Age,' so to speak...which ended with the onset of World War I. In the USA, the age was spoken of as 'The Gilded Age.' In Britain, it was called the 'Victorian Age.' All these names were an attempt to give name to the changes in the air with the coming of the twentieth century. In Berlin, the cabarets were wild and crazy—while in Paris, the Bohemian life-styles manifested themselves in a new glamour in the cabarets of Montmartre." Slottman, hesitated, cleared his throat, and resumed:

"Inspector, please forgive me for digressing, but I wanted to 'set the stage' for what I feel has befallen Mr. Vallinsky. His is a curious case, indeed. Oh, I feel that he's a dangerous person, but I also think that he has been 'used' so to speak, by certain criminal elements in Russia, elements outside the circle of the Intelligence community—as you are aware, certain 'agents' who are considered to be trustworthy by the intelligentsia, have proven, time and again, to be untrustworthy, and some have not only crossed the line, but have committed murder, theft, espionage, you name it. I'm not fully convinced that Victor Vallinsky is guilty of crimes against the Motherland...What I _am_ convinced of, is that he is a conduit, albeit possibly an unwillingly conduit, to the Russian mafia—those involved in art thefts—particularly, masterpieces of art—therefore, it is not to be considered a national security matter, but rather, a criminal enterprise resulting in significant 'financial sector' problems; problems for France, as well as for perhaps Austria, and maybe even Germany.

Why do I think this is possible? It has to do with his daughter, Laura Vallinsky. As I mentioned, she is in New York at this time, but I have information that leads me to believe that she may be in danger from certain of the Russian mafia—a fringe group, not interested in the cause of mother Russia, but involved in the cause of theft—an international, far-reaching global ring of criminals who specialize in theft in the art community. This is a little out of our normal duties, foremost of which is the security of France. In your case, it may blur the line between criminal cases and intelligence/security case. I digress—forgive me.

The bottom line: We need to know WHO the contacts in the Russian mafia are, names, addresses, whatever you can get from Victor. It is important that we obtain this information as soon as possible—we do know that there is something brewing, a major art theft is in the planning—we, of course, do not know where it might be. The theft could be anywhere in Europe or North America, or elsewhere, for all we know; however, <u>something</u> is brewing—something huge. See what you can find out from Mr. Vallinsky, and get back to me. Do not hesitate to contact me with any questions whatsoever. In any event, my best regards to you and your fellow countrymen.

Signed: Pierre Tomas, Paris, France

Inspector Fellner didn't bother to glance in the direction of his prisoner as he turned on his heel and barked at Johan Slottman, "Lock him up—we'll talk again tomorrow—eight am sharp. He goes back to France tomorrow night—if the Russians get to him, may God have pity on his soul..."

CHAPTER 9

Dax thought back to his first 'real' date with Laura—it had been about one week after they first met at Starbucks. Laura had wanted to see a movie; however, Dax had wanted to make it a 'special' evening—one that she'd never forget. After mulling it over in his head for two days, he finally hit on just the right thing to do—Sunday Brunch in Central Park, followed with a matinee at the Art Cinema just off 42nd & Park Avenue in Manhattan. A MAN AND A WOMAN, one of Dax's favorites was playing—a 1966 French film starring Anouk Aimee and Jean-Louis Trintignant. He had seen it years earlier, back in St Louis when he was about seventeen. A great love story with a fantastic sound-track—guaranteed to put you into a mood for romance—particularly if you were lucky enough to be with someone like Laura...

The evening was even better than he had hoped—Laura loved the dinner, adored the movie, and, he hoped, moved closer to loving him. Dax knew that he was in love, only he wasn't so sure about Laura's feelings for him. She was an enigma within an enigma—but then, aren't <u>all</u> women? Of course, the female species are all mystery girls—mysteries even to themselves; sometimes, <u>most</u> of all, mysteries to themselves...

CHAPTER 10

Laura was convinced that she wasn't going to escape from her captors. She had come to the conclusion that there was absolutely nothing she could do to free herself. She felt that she was totally in the control of these gangsters. And, there was nothing else she could tell them that would satisfy their curiosity—she knew that they were convinced that she was covering up for her dad and was not telling them everything. But, the fact is, she had answered every question they had thrown at her, and she didn't evade any questions—when she told them she didn't know, it was because she <u>did</u> <u>not</u> know—end of story.

But now that she was at the end of her rope, so to speak, she mentally went through her options—there weren't many—in fact, there weren't <u>any</u> viable options; however, she racked her brain trying to come up with <u>something</u>, no matter how slim the chance that it would work; just when she had almost given up hope, fate intervened...

"Laura, get up!" barked Mikael. In the dark she hadn't seen him walk up to her cage.

"Okay—let me see if I can stand—I've been squatted down for so long I don't know whether my legs will hold me up..."

Mikael shot an ugly sneer at her and snarled, "Quit whining and get the hell up—NOW!"

"I'm okay—just a sec...' Laura cried out as she forced herself to stand. Her wobbly legs trembled, but held fast.

"Good girl—Theo, get that lock open and let's go!"

"You got it, Mikael—we'll be good-to-go in a minute."

Laura tried to step out of her confined space, couldn't lift her left foot enough to clear the obstacles in her path, lost her balance, and flung her out-stretched arms toward Mikael. The look in his eyes told her everything—those coal-black eyes stared at her—it couldn't have been more than a micro-second, and yet, in that fraction of an instant, she knew an ancient truth—this was a man—no, not a man, an <u>animal</u> who would not hesitate to snuff her life out as casually as if he were yawning. Laura's head hit the solid wood flooring with a sickening thud—she sprawled spread-eagle across the floor, crimson blood from her head-wound spilled onto the beige carpeting within seconds.

Mikael screamed at his two stooges, "What the fuck are you waitin' for—pick her up, dumb-asses!"

The two henchmen grasped Laura and brought her to her feet. Laura's head hung down as the blood continued to flow.

"Are you two idiots going to do anything about the blood?" Mikael asked, his face now purple with rage.

"Don't worry about it, boss—we got it covered. "Peter, grab her ankles—I got her wrists—let's go!" The trio scampered down the stairs and out the back door of their 'loaner' house—in two minutes time they were out of the city limits and headed to Manhattan.

CHAPTER 11

"Hey, cornet man, play us a tune," shouted one of the Blue Moon regulars who had seen Dax with his horn.

"Anything in particular, Sonny?' asked Dax as he blew a few warm-up notes on his beloved Courtois Cornet.

"Hell, I like it all...you're the maestro, pick one of your faves—okay?"

"You got it—give me a couple of minutes and I'll jump into one of the best ones you'll ever hear," Dax replied, a forced grin on his face. It had now been almost two weeks since Laura's disappearance, and he was at his wit's end— he had decided that there was only one thing to do—go to the NYPD, maybe even the FBI, if that's what it took to get something going—he just knew that the time had long-since passed for him to sit and do nothing but worry...Laura's life was in danger—if she wasn't already a murder victim. Then there was the possibility that she could have been kidnapped and taken to Europe, or elsewhere—the hell of it was that she could be <u>anywhere!</u>

Dax forced himself to tear into an old Chet Baker standard, 'TIME AFTER TIME,' first recorded by Baker in 1954, then again in 1964. Dax was not known for his vocals, but this trac required a vocal and his one singer was not available, so he gave it his best shot—he managed to get through the vocals, but the fuse was lit when he launched into his cornet solo...just the night before a jazz fan at the Blue Moon, after listening to Dax's cool rendering of this song, remarked to Dax, "Man, that horn of yours is so languid, hell, not just languid—I mean the smoothest and softest sounds I've ever heard—I could have mistaken it for a harp—if I hadn't just watched you play that cornet... great job, Dax!"

"Thanks! Well, I do have to admit to one thing—I switched to my E(flat) soprano horn for that solo—hits a higher register than the B(flat) cornet...anyway, really glad you liked it."

Dax decided, as his gig was ending at the Blue Moon, that he had to talk to the mysterious blonde, Greta. The gal with no last name, a dancer with Laura at the off-Broadway venue. As he walked out the door of the Blue Moon, he knew in his heart-of-hearts that he would have to find out what Greta knew—if anything, about Laura's disappearance. The woman of mystery had assured Dax that she'd let him know should she hear from Laura, but in every call to her, the message never varied, and it went something like this:"No, Dax, I haven't heard anything. Yes, Dax, I will let you know the minute I hear anything." However, this time, Greta added, for good measure, the following quip: "Dax, you don't know much about Laura—she's a strange girl, and she keeps things to herself—guess it's the way she was brought up...anyway, I understand why you're worried, and I'm worried as well...Bye!"

CHAPTER 12

Greta was, once again, seated at her favorite watering hole, The Shades, nursing a vodka & tonic. She didn't look up as Dax Bolton waltzed up to the bar and dropped onto the bar stool next to her. "Well, fancy meeting you here, Miss Greta. Any news from Laura—anything at all?" asked Dax, the tension in his voice noticeable to the couple sitting near the bar at a table for two.

"Hello, Dax. No, I haven't heard a word from Laura—I do think it's past time that something needs to be done—don't you think you need to turn in a missing person's report to the police?"

"Well, when we talked about that earlier, you advised against it—why the change of heart now?" asked Dax.

"Earlier, in my opinion, I didn't see it as a matter of life or death—now, I don't know, but it just doesn't feel good—I mean, when it's been this long, anything could have happened, and most of that would not be good..."

"I agree—first thing in the morning I'm going to turn in a missing person report on Laura—I need to give your name to the NYPD as a person who, at least, knows Laura and has worked with her. Okay?"

"Certainly—no problem."

"Well, I will need to know your last name—you never gave me the benefit of that bit of information—"

"Didn't I? Sorry about that, Dax. Sometimes a girl forgets, I guess. It's Hammett. Hammet is my last name—

yeah, just like the writer, Dashiell Hammett...isn't that what you wanted to know?"

"Yeah, it is—thanks for letting me know. Is there anything else I can tell the police when I turn in the report tomorrow?"

"Well, you can give them the name of the man who hired Laura—his name is Harry Lime, and I know that he has background information regarding Laura—don't know if that's something that will be helpful or not, but I suppose anything is better than nothing..."

"Greta, you got that right. Try hard to remember if there is anything, anything at all you can give me that might help—"

"Well, there *is* one thing—"

"What thing?"

Greta Hammett grimaced and forced a smile toward Dax, cleared her throat and began, "Well, it might be important to let the NYPD know about her dad and the 'troubles' in which he, apparently, is involved."

"You mean with the so-called Russian mafia?"

"Well, I don't know if there is any basis in fact about the Russian mafia, but he has a real problem—of course, Laura never specifically gave me the lowdown, but I could tell from her comments, here and there, that she was worried sick about him. Laura even confided in me once that she didn't know if she'd ever see her father alive again..."

"Well, that's news—she never told me that—I mean, I know there's trouble, but she never made it sound as if it were something he wouldn't survive...however, I did get a vibe that she was also worried about herself, to some extent—she never specifically said, "I'm afraid for my life, Dax. But, putting all the pieces of the puzzle together—at least the parts I'm privy to, something doesn't add up...I have a really bad feeling that whatever's happened <u>must</u> have a connection to the trouble her dad is in."

"Yes, Dax, I feel the same way. Say, I'm bushed—got to call it a night. Do me a favor and let me know what the NYPD has to say, and let them know I'd be glad to answer any questions they may have in regard to Laura—good night, Dax."

CHAPTER 13

Dax was worried—he didn't know how to approach the NYPD with the news of Laura's disappearance. He knew that he had waited too long, desperately hoping against hope that his fears were unfounded and that she was just 'playing hooky' so to speak, and doing her own thing for a few days...Wait a second! That doesn't hold water, does it, Dax, ole boy? Why wouldn't she at least call you, or call Greta, or their boss at the theatre? Her job <u>does</u> depend upon showing up for work, does it not?

The more he thought about it, the more he was convinced that he had waited too damn long to go to the cops. For starters, he would not be able to explain the situation regarding Victor Vallinsky, Laura's dad, who supposedly was in serious trouble in Europe...the story would sound to the NYPD like an amateur screenplay for a really bad movie... anyway, Laura had made him promise not to go off half-cocked if she doesn't return. Dax knew that she <u>must</u> have anticipated a problem—he wished to hell she had confided more in him than she had before she left for Trenton.

Dax finally decided that perhaps she was worried he'd be in trouble as well...then again, what did Dax <u>really</u> know about Laura—other than the fact that he was in love with her—more so every day that went by...

Dax knew he couldn't put off the visit to the NYPD any longer. He knew he'd have to pull himself together and make the trek to Manhattan's Precinct 13...he grabbed his jacket and rushed out of his apartment onto the streets of Manhattan.

CHAPTER 14

The trip to NYPD Precinct 13 hadn't gone well. In fact, it had been, in Dax's opinion, an unmitigated disaster. Not only was the officer assigned to take Dax's statement indifferent to the matter of a missing German national who had seemingly disappeared, he was openly hostile to this cocky jazz musician giving the missing person account. Once back in the confines of his apartment, Dax re-wound the 'interrogation' through his mind, and it went something like this...

PRECINCT 13—NYPD—MANHATTAN

"I'd like to report a missing person."

DESK DUTY Sergeant Mulholland looked up from his newspaper and stared stonily at the man standing in front of him and growled, "Just a minute, sir. Let me get the form I need for your report—want to make sure we don't leave any pertinent information off the report—okay with you?"

Dax answered, "of course," as the sergeant was already reaching into the desk behind him for the papers he wanted. "All right, let's start at the beginning, shall we...first off, I need your full name."

"Dax Bolton."

"If I may ask, what is your relationship to the person of interest?"

"We're dating—I've only known her for a few days..."

"Name of the person of interest?"
"Laura. Laura Vallinsky."
"Address?"
"1151 Milton Place—Apt 33, Manhattan."
"Age?"
"Not sure on that—early 30s..."
"Her occupation?"
"Dancer"
"Is this Laura Vallinsky employed at this time?"
"Yes, she is in the cast of a new off-Broadway show scheduled to open in about three weeks—
"Name of her employer?"
"I'm not sure—I can give you the name and cell for the choreographer of the production—he's the one who hired Laura—
"And that is?"
"Let me dig out my iPhone contact list—just a sec...oh, here it is—Harry Lime, ph 212-335-7723..."
"Name of theatre where they are rehearsing?"
"Uh, let's see, I've been there a couple of time—uh, here it is...The Lyric—that's it—The Lyric Theatre—funny name for a theatre isn't it..."
"How long has Miss Vallinsky been missing?"
"Well, going on two weeks now—I wanted to contact the NYPD earlier, but..."
"Why <u>didn't</u> you contact us sooner? Two weeks is a long time for a person to be missing..."
"I know, I know. Before Laura left for Trenton she told me that although her trip was planned for only two days, it was possible that she may have to stay in the Trenton area a little longer than that—that's all she said..."

"I see," said Sergeant Mulholland. "What else? Tell me everything you know about whom she was going to see, where she was staying, everything...okay?" the Sergeant asked, his voice cloaked with suspicion...

"Sergeant, let me give you a little background on Laura before we get into that—all right?"

"Sure, Mr. Bolton, whatever you say..."

"Okay—thanks—here goes. Laura lived for many years in Berlin, Germany. And, I understand that her father is apparently in some sort of 'difficulty' in eastern Europe, the nature of which Laura hasn't confided in me; however, I do know that it must be a serious matter because she is so tight-lipped on the subject of her father. The only thing I've managed to learn is that her dad, Victor Vallinsky, is apparently being blackmailed by some shady types in Russia—according to Laura, she thinks these characters are involved in the Russian Mafia..."

"Russian Mafia?" Are you serious, Mr. Bolton? And how would she know about this activity—is this Laura involved in criminal activity as well?"

"NO! I'm sure of that!"

"How can you be so sure—you've just told me that you've only known Laura for a short time—and, all you've told me so far is that she's a dancer, she's rehearsing for a theatrical piece at an off-Broadway venue—

Dax looked at the sergeant as if he wanted to strangle him, stifled his thoughts, forced a smile and began anew...

"Laura left exactly ten days ago on the noon train from Grand Central Station to Trenton, New Jersey—her plan was to stay in the Trenton area for two days and then return to New York. However, she <u>did</u> tell me not to worry if she were to be delayed in her return—she did <u>not</u> tell me that I would not hear from her...well, I haven't heard a word from Laura, and I've left over two dozen cell phone calls which she has not returned. Sergeant, this is most definitely <u>not</u> like Laura—I'm worried sick about her..."

"Another thing you haven't told me yet, Mr. Bolton, is just this—what was the nature of her visit to Trenton? I mean, was she just taking a couple days off, a vacation, work-related, what?"

"I was just getting to that—she would not tell me who she was meeting with—but she did tell me that it had 'something to do with her father'. My gut feeling is that the person or persons unknown she was meeting could be affiliated with the so-called Russian Mafia group she mentioned, or an opposing splinter group from Europe—in any event, most likely gangsters of some stripe...could be enemies of the particular Russian Mafia group that her father, Victor Vallinsky, has apparently run afoul of..."

"Hmm, that does make for an interesting scenario, does it not? Tell you what, Mr. Bolton—I'm going to take a few minutes and type this report—then I'll ask you to sign it, I'll pass it to Lieutenant Burk, and he'll be contacting you. Okay?"

"Sure thing, Sergeant Mulholland—thanks for your time—it may be nothing, but I've got a really bad feeling that something is very wrong..."

"Well, we'll find out what's up—and I'm sure we'll have more questions for you, so its most important that you keep in touch—by the way, as they say in the movies, 'don't leave town without checking in with the NYPD first,' okay? By the way, you can wait in the coffee room, just off to your right—have a cup of coffee, and the detective will be with you shortly. Sound good?"

"You bet—thanks!"

CHAPTER 14

Dax had fallen asleep while nursing his coffee inside the Precinct 13 break-room. He was slumped over the table and began to faintly snore. Suddenly, Sergeant Mulholland shook his shoulder to awaken him from his slumber. "Hey, Mr. Bolton—the detective is ready to see you. All right?"

"Sorry about that, Sergeant. I've had almost no sleep the past few days—plus, I play cornet at the Blue Moon over in Brooklyn—ever heard of it? Jazz spot that attracts jazz lovers from all the boroughs of New York…"

"Can't say that I have. Then again, I'm strictly a country & western fan—also like that ole-time rock & roll…"

Dax managed a slight smile and replied, "Yeah, I like that stuff as well, but jazz, with a little blues thrown in for good measure, and I'm good to go…anyway, we play three nights a week, and the Blue Moon doesn't close 'til the wee hours…so, sleep is a rare commodity, plus I'm worried sick about Laura, as you can imagine…"

"Detective Burk is in room # 25, just down the hall—he's waiting on you right now—better get a move on," the Duty Sergeant said, his timbre of his voice somewhat less strident to Dax than during his interrogation just an hour earlier.

Dax hustled down the hall, saw the name, Detective Allison Burk, NYPD, emblazoned on the door to office #25. Dax stopped, knocked once on the door and immediately a voice boomed, 'C'mon in, Mr. Bolton. Grab a chair and let's talk, shall we?"

Dax shook hands with the detective and was amazed at the size of the man—Detective Burk stood at least six foot six, with a body-builder's build, brownish-blonde hair which was closely-cropped—dark navy suit, buttoned-down Ivy League-style dress shirt—hell, he looked more like a Wall Street Tycoon than a detective, thought Dax.

"Pleased to meet you, Detective Burk," Dax stammered as he shook hands with the man.

"Sit, please, Mr. Bolton. Looks like we've got some urgent business to discuss here...

THIRTY MINUTES LATER...

"So, Dax, I think we understand each other—do we not?" asked Lt Burk.

"Well, I <u>hope</u> that is the case—at first, I wasn't sure where we were headed..."

"I understand, Dax. This <u>is</u> an unusual situation, wouldn't you agree?"

Dax fixed a long stare at Lt Burk, then said, "Yes, it is unusual. I don't have someone I'm in love with disappear without a trace every day of the week—in fact, this is the first time anything like this has happened to me. Maybe you guys deal with stuff like this all the time, but for me, it's a new ballgame..."

"Of course it is—and, no, we don't see cases like this very often, but let me say this...I still don't understand why you waited so long to make this report, but for now I'll buy your story...however, that said, I don't like it—in fact, there's a whole laundry list of things I don't like about this thing—

"For instance?" asked Dax.

"First of all, starting with your story of the Russian Mafia being involved...well, that's a stretch. Secondly, there's the matter of Laura Vallinsky herself—what in the hell do we know about her—<u>you</u> don't really seem to know much about her. And, she certainly isn't on our radar—at least not yet. We're going to make inquiries with both the FBI and the CIA in regard to Laura, as well as her dad, Victor Vallinsky."

Lieutenant Burk waited for a response from Dax, got none and continued, "This matter may already be out of my hands and I don't even know it yet...let's be agreed on this, if nothing else: Number One: You don't leave town without an okay from the NYPD; Number Two: I can't be certain that you've told me all you know, so I'll have to dig deeper into the backgrounds of the vanished lady, Laura Vallinsky, as well as her papa, Victor Vallinsky. Number Three: I don't like you, Dax. No, that's not it, exactly. I don't believe your story—at least not all of it...hell, don't let that concern you too damn much. I don't trust a lot of folks—particularly when they feed me what has all the makings of a 'cloak and dagger' story...who knows, maybe you're telling me everything, but my money says it ain't so...in fact, you may know a hell of a lot more than what you've told me. What do you think of that, Dax?"

Dax's face turned purple with anger and he felt flushed as he struggled to contain his temper.

"Aw, hell, Dax, don't take it so hard. I'm paid to be suspicious—hell, I don't even trust my own mother, and she brought me into this world...how 'bout them apples?" Detective Burk asked as his face instantly metamorphosed from a sneer to a smile.

"Listen, Dax, here's the God's truth: I've worked cases where, in the end, after weeks of working our butts off, checking out every possible lead, interviewing every locatable witness, prying the truth from folks who aren't on the best of terms with the truth—some of them wouldn't know the truth if it hit them in the face...well, after all that work, after all that time, the bad-guy turns out to be the one who filed the missing person report...surprised, Dax? Don't be—it's the truth. Don't be unduly concerned with my suspicions—like I said, I get paid to be suspicious. Should I go on, or do we understand each other?" Dax felt as if he had taken a sucker punch in the gut—his head was spinning as he whispered, "Yeah, we understand each other."

"Good day, Mr. Bolton. We'll be in touch," Detective Burk stood and smiled for the first time since Dax entered the detective's office. They shook hands, and in a heartbeat, Dax was out the door.

CHAPTER 15

Dax was mad—he had gone through the third-degree with the NYPD when he reported Laura missing, had been interrogated as if he were the perpetrator of a crime because he had waited several days to make a missing persons report, and he now felt that his life was under the microscope of the NYPD, maybe even the FBI and CIA, and who knows what else...Homeland Security?

In any event, he was worried about what he did NOT know about the mysterious Greta Hammett—well, her last name wasn't Garbo, but he couldn't help but think of the 1930s and 1940s iconic actress when he thought of Greta. He decided to have a talk with Laura's boss, Harry Lime, the choreographer at the Lyric Theatre who had hired Laura. Of course, he had also hired Greta for the up-coming theatrical piece, working title: AT LONG LAST GLOIRE. Dax had already had several conversations with Harry Lime—but those conversations had dealt only with Laura—now he wanted to find out all he could about Greta Hammett...

AN HOUR LATER—LYRIC THEATRE, MANHATTAN

"Thanks for seeing me on such short notice, Mr. Lime," said Dax Bolton as the two men shook hands.

"Oh, no problem whatsoever—I needed a break anyway... what's up with Laura? Any word—<u>anything</u> at all?"

"No—that's why I wanted to speak with you personally, rather than our customary cell phone chats..."

"I understand—it's good that we are meeting face-to-face. What can I tell you?"

"Well, you already know that Laura and I have been acquainted but a short time—yet I'm already crazy about her and not knowing anything is driving me around the bend, as the saying goes..."

"Certainly. I'm worried sick myself—Laura is a fantastic dancer—trained in Berlin and Paris, as I believe you already know..."

"Yeah—she's told me about that. Her dad insisted that she get the best training available—Laura's mother died giving birth to Laura, and the old man wanted Laura to realize the un-fulfilled dreams of Mrs. Vallinsky, who was a world-class dancer in her own right..."

"Yes, actually, believe it or not, I had heard of her mother—well, not directly, but my mother was a dancer also, and she kept up with the big names—it's really a fairly small universe—ballet and even the modern dance require so much of the dancers, male and female, that they almost have no life outside the dance world, and it becomes suffocating sometimes...one gives up a lot for the dance, but then, if one has the talent, and the grit, and the good fortune to continue, it tops everything—maybe even love itself—because, as you can appreciate, the discipline doesn't leave much time to devote to romantic dalliances..."

"I'm sure that's true—Laura has mentioned that a few times—I think that's one reason she's non-committal on the romance thing—I've told her, right out, that I'm in love with her, but when I tried to get a read for how she feels about me, well, I'm batting zero there..."

"Don't feel like you're alone—countless thousands of suitors the world over have experienced exactly what you're feeling...

Say, what in particular can I help you with?"

"Well, Harry, if I may call you Harry..."

"Of course. Shoot."

"Okay—here it is...has Laura mentioned anything at all to you about 'difficulties' her father may be experiencing in Eastern Europe, or in Russia? Anything at all?"

"Well, she has left a couple of innuendos, so to speak, about her dad, and her voice always grew guarded on those few times when she mentioned him, but the instant I began to ask any questions or show any interest, she cut the conversation short—no dice—it appeared to be an 'off-limits' subject...okay?"

"I suspected that might be the case, but thanks for clearing that up. It's just that I fear that Laura's disappearance may have something to do with her father's troubles, whatever they may be."

"I don't have a clue—is there anything else I can help you with? My dancers will be coming back from their short break in a few minutes."

"Actually, there's another reason I'm here...would you mind letting me know, in confidence, what you know about Greta Hammett? I know that she is one of your dancers and that she is a friend of Laura's...as always, appreciate anything you can tell me."

"Why do you want to know, Dax?"

"Well, at this point, anything about Greta could be important—she is, as far as I know, Laura's only friend in New York City that I'm aware of...other than yourself, of course," Dax said. A forced grin made a slow trek across his face. It was the first time Dax had smiled since the day Laura left New York.

"Dax, I really have nothing to add, I don't think—wait a second, maybe there is something I can tell you...it may be nothing, then again, who can say...anyway, on the day that Laura left for her engagement in Trenton, Greta took sick about noon, had to leave rehearsal in a hurry, and I believe ended up at Mercy Hospital for a short stay...don't know what it was about and she wouldn't discuss it, other than to say 'oh, it was nothing—must have been something I ate—and changed the subject. Greta was back at work the next day and worked like a dog—the girl must have a cast-iron constitution, as well as being a wonderfully trained and fit pro-dancer...that's all I can tell you...Oh, almost forgot—the girl has top-notch recommendations from her prior employers..."

"One last question, Harry, has Greta ever worked, as a dancer, in Europe?"

"Hmm, it's not on her resume, and don't recall her bringing that up—that's something that normally would be at the top of a resume, so my guess is no, she hasn't danced professionally out of the United States, at least not to my knowledge. Okay?"

"Yes—thanks, and of course, should you hear anything at all, about Laura, please let me know asap—thanks!" Dax smiled as he bid adieu to Harry Lime.

"No problem, Mr. Bolton. I'll be in touch the minute I do hear something—have a good day," stammered Harry Lime as he greeted the first of his dancers returning from their break.

CHAPTER 16

Mikael knew he had screwed up badly. Not only had he allowed Laura to hurt herself, he had been stupid enough to take her to an emergency room just outside Trenton, New Jersey. Trenton, for God's sake! He should have realized that, number one, in order to be treated at an emergency room at a metropolitan hospital, anywhere in the U.S.A., you'd have to not only furnish proof of insurance, you'd also be forced to show driver's license, home address, phone numbers, ad infinitum...oh, hell yes, they had 'fake' papers for Laura, but the problem wasn't the papers—the real problem was just this—Mikael knew that a missing person's report would eventually go out on 'the network' of the various law enforcement agencies, including, of course, the FBI, NYPD, and God knows who the hell else...

Mikael knew that the odds were good, hell, they were 100% <u>guaranteed</u>—to make a 'hit' somewhere along the way...so, the solution, the <u>only</u> solution—was to get the hell out of Dodge, and soon, very soon...

Mikael had a plan, and that plan would be put into operation once they arrived safely back in mother Russia... he would know precisely which line of action to take, just as he always knew which course of action would put him in harm's way. He had studied the 'game plan,' he had worked too hard, to lose it all now...now that he was so close, so close to realizing all his sleazy dreams...by God, he'd been given the short end of the stick by every sorry son of a bitch he'd encountered in his twenty year 'career' with the Russian mafia 'family.'

He wasn't going to risk everything for no reason—there had to be a reason if he was going to risk being caught in the cross-hairs of his fellow gangsters' sights. He'd make sure that, if things went bad, real bad, he'd have a back-up plan, a plan guaranteed to put him on 'easy street,' out of harm's way...that was the way it had been programmed for him by 'Popsie,' all those years ago when he gladly took all the shit assignments, took abuse from the big bosses, took it all, like a man,—he never complained, would not cry, no matter how much he hurt...the truth of it was, Mikael hurt all the time. When your youth is spent on the mean streets of a Russian province—when a daily ritual is to regularly be thrashed to within an inch of your life—beaten for any transgression, no matter how trivial, no matter how inconsequential, it does things to you. Yes, it 'toughens' you up, makes you a dangerous hombre. However, the toughness comes with a price. And, the price you pay is the loss of your soul. Your only consolation is just this—the pain makes you a legitimate player; someone others learn to leave alone. They were afraid to mess with Mikael. His fellow mobsters had left him alone for the past few years... Mikael thought that it was possibly due to several corpses he'd left behind. Hell, he'd lost count of guys who thought they were smarter, or tougher, than Mikeal...in the end, they were all wrong—dead wrong...

CHAPTER 17

Detective Allison Burk was on edge. He hadn't received any word back on the whereabouts of Laura Vallinsky. And, he had done everything he knew to do, and he'd done it by the book. Detective Burk was good at his job—very good. The bureaucratic red tape involving a foreign-national missing person report to the Federal Agencies was mind-boggling. And, he knew that the case file for Laura Vallinsky would be thick enough to make the reading of Leo Tolstoy's classic <u>WAR AND PEACE</u> seem like child's play.

Detective Burk always operated by the book—and the book's rules were very precise, very concrete, not easily misunderstood—that was the way he liked it. It had always been important to Allison Burk that he knew precisely what was expected of him, that he knew <u>precisely</u> how to accomplish his objective, whether it be at work or on personal business. So, now that the Feds were involved in what he thought of as 'the German Girl Case,' the Feds would not let him do his job.

Detective Burk knew in his heart-of-hearts that most likely they would never find Laura Vallinsky alive. Oh, he didn't have anything on which to base this gut feeling—other than his iron-clad intuition. And, that intuition had never failed—not once in the fifteen years he'd been on the force; and, by God, it was not going to fail him this time. Not when this could be his lucky break...the teen-age Allison Burk had nursed a secret ambition—he had always wanted to one day be District Attorney for the City of New York. Only problem was, he had dropped out of law school after completing only one year...so, naturally, being a realist, Detective Burk had come up with Plan B. He knew that Plan B would be the game-changer...this bitch, this Laura Vallinsky, bless her German soul, was going to be the conduit to all his dreams...

CHAPTER 18

Dax suspected something was wrong...he had just pulled up a voicemail from Detective Burk of the NYPD, and he didn't like what he heard. He was so taken aback by the message that he hit the 'play' button one more time, to ensure that he had heard correctly..."Mr. Bolton, Lt Burke here—got some news for you, and it's not good—better come on down to the precinct and we'll talk—I'll be here all day, but the sooner the better...thanks!"

What the hell? If it was bad news, why hadn't he told me, wondered Dax. The son of a bitch is playing games, and they're not to my liking, but I've got to play ball with his rule book, not mine...why didn't he tell me what he knows, and get it over with...

In less than fifteen minutes, Dax strode into Precinct 13, Manhattan Office, and asked for Detective Burk. "And who are you, sir?" asked the Desk Sergeant.

"Dax Bolton. I'm here at Detective Burk's request—he said it was urgent. It's in regard to the missing persons report on Laura Vallinsky..."

"Vallinsky?! Why didn't you say so—c'mon, I'll escort you to Burk's office," replied the sergeant.

Detective Burk met Dax at the door. "Dax! C'mon in—sit down and let's talk. Okay?"

Dax dropped onto the chair in front of Burk's desk, and, unable to mask the irritation and desperation in his voice, asked, "Why couldn't you tell me on the cell the news you have? I've been going nuts these past few minutes on the way over here—"

"Sorry 'bout that, Dax. Couldn't be helped. Here's the scoop—I'm afraid it's not good news...let me re-phrase that—it's not the kind of news I wanted to give you about Miss Vallinsky, but let's not jump to any unpleasant conclusions, at least until..."

"Until <u>what</u>, Burk? What gives? I need to know, and I need to know now!"

"Uh, I understand—okay, here goes...we've been advised by the Intelligence Community..."

"You mean the FBI and/or CIA?" asked Dax.

"Well, I can't get into that just now—let it suffice to say that several agencies have been involved in the investigation—particularly due to the 'situation' with her dad, in Russia. I can't give you any specifics regarding the status of our inquiries, but I can tell you that we've been in contact with French, Austrian, and German Intelligence Agencies, as well as an informal 'connection,' if you will, to underground contacts familiar with the so-called 'Russian Mafia.'

A nasty business, that...I digress. Here's what we know: Laura is apparently out of the country—our guess is that she's in Russia, or elsewhere in Eastern Europe. Laura is, as you know, a German citizen, and was here on a work permit, or temporary visa, so she is not a U.S. citizen, as you are aware. Hence, we are limited in what we can do in the investigation—however, since she was apparently abducted against her will, and that abduction took place on American soil, we do have some jurisdiction in her disappearance. Bottom line is this: She's out of the U.S., we don't know where, precisely, she is. An investigation is on-going, involving both the U.S. Intelligence community, as well as several European agencies. This situation involves more than just a missing young lady...don't get me wrong, we want Laura found, safe and sound, just as you do, but there are 'bigger fish to fry,' so to speak, in this scenario..."

"So, where does that leave us, here in New York—dumb, and not so happy..." asked Dax, the bitterness and hopelessness apparent in his hoarse voice.

"I don't like it, either, Dax. Sorry to have to give you the bad news; however, the good news is that, as far as we know, she's still alive and apparently well, although we do have a report that she was injured, rather severely, in an accident, as it were, in New Jersey before the perps left the country, flying out of JFK."

"Well, thanks for that. And, thanks for bringing me up-to-date, Burk. What do we do now? Or, rather, what do I do now?"

"Nothing. There is absolutely nothing you can do at this point in time. Tell you what—try to get it off your mind if you can, it's out of my hands, out of your hands, all we can do is wait—I know its not easy, but that's the way it is..."

"Wait a second, Burk. You haven't told me how the Feds figured all this out...what are you not telling me?"

Detective Burk, for the first time, looked flustered." You know everything about the case that I know—trust me, Dax. I know it's hard, particularly with this thing going Federal on us—it was an international situation from the beginning. Of course, there was no way in hell you would have known any of this—other than the little that Laura confided in you. Oh, almost forgot: did you get any information from Laura's fellow dancer, this, uh, Greta, something or other..."

"Well, nothing of importance. I got very little information from her—they are friends, they've worked together as dancers, but that's about it...do you, Detective Burk, have anything on Greta? Anything at all?"

"No, nothing—clean as a whistle, as far as we know."

"All right—keep me posted if you hear anything new." Dax said as he left Precinct 13, and walked, in solitude, to his apartment.

CHAPTER 19

 Dax knew he had to leave New York. It made no real sense. Yet it had to happen. He'd called New York City home for over ten years, and it almost felt like home. Almost. He wouldn't be abandoning Laura—Laura was gone and he didn't know whether he'd ever see her again. No one, least of all Dax, knew whether Laura was dead or alive…Detective Burk had kept Dax marginally informed—of course, that information consisted of precisely this: "Dax, nothing new to report—no news of Laura or her whereabouts—the underground contacts have apparently dried-up, or have been bought off, in any event, there is nothing floating out there, news-wise…" Dax wondered whether the mighty USA had been bought-off, or whether there had been some kind of 'arrangement' made in which the USA would 'look the other way,' in regard to the status of Laura Vallinsky—after all, she wasn't even an American citizen—she was German, her father an Austrian with a questionable pedigree of international criminal associates…

 It really was no wonder that Dax had heard nothing new of Laura—it had now been three months since she disappeared. And, on top of that, the Lyric's show had been canceled after one week and the one connection he had to Laura, in the form of Greta, was lost as she had also left New York without a word to Dax. He had been bitter about that at first, but as time went by, he thought about Greta less and less, finally decided that her connection to Laura appeared to be inconsequential—whether, in the long run, that turned out not to be the case, he didn't have a clue.

And, his new home would be California. The Golden State—at least that's what it had been billed over a good part of the twentieth century; however, as America entered the early years of the twenty-first century, California seemed to have lost some of its glitter. Well, to Dax, on the one occasion he had visited California, in the 1990s, it had been golden to him. He had been lucky enough to hook up with a premier cornet & trumpet maestro of the cool California School of Jazz, by the name of Jumpin' Salestro, or 'Jump,' for short. Jump had taken Dax under his wing for a short time, and had turned Dax into a virtuoso cornet player.

Dax had intended to stay in California, but an unfortunate series of events changed all that: Jump died of a drug overdose; then Dax got strung out on alcohol, ending a lucrative long-term gig at the casinos in Reno & Lake Tahoe, Nevada. Now that Laura was apparently lost, and likely lost for good, Dax knew it was time—past time—to move on. "California, here I come," Dax, whispered to himself. He knew he'd have to clear it with Detective Burk at Precinct 13, and hoped it wouldn't put the Blue Moon in too big a funk, but he was going, and that was that…

CHAPTER 20

It took Dax precisely three weeks to tie-up loose ends in New York and finalize plans for his California move. He had decided on San Diego—actually, San Diego had been decided <u>for</u> him...that is, fate had, once again, reached out to him and practically made the decision for him...

ONE WEEK EARLIER...

The professional jazz world is a small world—a universe unto itself...and, Dax was a known cornet maestro throughout the hot spots of jazz, California, Chicago, New Orleans...So, when Dax made a few calls to his contacts, the word spread quickly that Dax Bolton was leaving New York and heading to California.

The phone rang in Dax's Manhattan apartment, he grabbed his cell and said "hello." A voice out of the past roared into the receiver..."Dax! Is that really you, man? What's up? Inquiring minds want (need) to know, brother..."

"Yes, this is Dax. Whom do I have the pleasure of speaking to..."

"Aw, man, you disappoint me—I'm your best bud in the world and you don't even recognize my voice...I'm hurt, man. Hurt real bad...ha-ha, just joking—hell, it's me, Roscoe. "

"Roscoe! Sorry I'm slow on the uptake—how the hell are you?" Dax asked.

"I'm cool, man. Cool. Just like the days of old—hell, better than the days of old—I'm off the sauce, off the gambling, and on to my music, and that's the whole enchilada for me, bro. How's it hanging for you?"

"Well, I'm headed for San Diego—"

"Hell, Dax, why do you think I'm calling? I <u>know</u> you're headed to Diego—what I mean is, why the heck didn't you let me know? Man, I'd have hooked you up with a full-time gig as soon as I got the word…you got somethin' lined up yet?"

"Well, I've got a couple of things to look into to, nothing firm, yet…"

"Well, hold your horses. How 'bout five nights a week, minimum of a grand, paid in cash every Friday night, plus free dining and booze 24/7, whether you're performing or not. And, a monthly bonus, depending on the amount of business the place does each month. So, there's a built-in incentive to bring in the jazz-lovers, and, of course, those that haven't yet been bitten by the jazz-bug…what do you think, bro?"

"Sounds good—you didn't tell me the name of your club—"

"The Tropicana West—heard of it?"

"Can't say that I have, but then, as you know, I've been in New York for almost ten years, so I'm a little 'out of the loop,' as far as the West Coast goes, doncha know…"

"Yeah, I understand. The Tropicana is a real happening place—you'll love it—I just know it! You don't have to let me know right now, but I'm telling you, you won't find a better situation than The Tropicana—why don't you sleep on it a couple of days and give me a call when you decide—okay?"

"You got it, Roscoe. By the way, I assume you've already got the go-ahead to hire me?"

"Would I be tantalizing you for nothin' bro...come on, you know me better than that—"

"All right—couple of days and I'll get back to you—appreciate the call and the offer. Look forward to catching up with you soon."

"Good deal—say, what is your scheduled arrival date in San Diego?"

"Well, it's not precise—few things I've got to iron out before I leave, but I'm shooting for late next week. I"ll let you know when my flight is set-up..."

"Flight? Not driving out, bro?"

"No car—hell, don't really need one in New York."

"Yeah, I know that's true—of course, as you will recall, California ain't like that—everything in this state revolves around transportation—in L.A., and certainly in Diego, you are what you drive, bro. See ya!"

CHAPTER 21

Dax had two things on his agenda before he could leave the Big Apple for good. And, number one on his 'hit-list,' was visiting with Detective Burk. This was most important due to the fact that he had been ordered by the NYPD not to leave New York City without notification to them. And, Dax knew only too well that Burk might not be in the mood to approve his leaving the city. But he had not forgotton Burk's comments in their initial meeting when Dax had gone to Precinct 13 to turn in the missing persons report on Laura. His mind replayed the conversation word-for-word:

"Who knows? Maybe you're telling me everything...in fact, you may know a lot more than what you're telling us... I'm paid to be suspicious. Hell, I don't even trust my own mother...I don't like you and I certainly don't trust you, Dax. Hell, don't let that bother you too much—I don't trust, or like, a lot of people...remember, don't leave town until I give you permission...got it?"

The other piece of business that Dax had to tidy up before he left the city was his last performance at the Blue Moon. The owner had made plans for it to be a special occasion—one that he wanted the hordes of fans of Dax Bolton to remember, long after Dax had left New York for good...and that performance was scheduled for tomorrow night, a Saturday night, and by God, Dax was going to make sure that it was going to be a Saturday night that none of the patrons of the Blue Moon would soon forget...

CHAPTER 22

Dax looked at his wrist-watch, noted the time: 10 pm, Friday night—just one day from his farewell performance at the Blue Moon. He knew that he had to prepare because he wanted it to be a night to remember—a night that no one there could forget Dax's music...he thought back to what had brought him to this crossroads in his life, and, as always, it started with the first time he heard Bix Beiderbeke play his cornet—he blew it like he was making love to that horn—it was as if that musical instrument were a life-line to the hereafter—a connection from the earthly life to the spirit life.

He had memorized most of the clippings he'd read over the years about Bix...and he remembered a reporter's quote from Octavio Paz, exactly as he'd seen it when he was only seventeen years old and had committed it to memory..."Life is imaginary, we bow to the tyranny of a phantom. Love is a privileged perception, the most total and lucid not only of the unreality of the world, but of our own unreality; we traverse a realm of shadows, we ourselves are shadows..."

The reporter had written: "Bix Beiderbecke, through the artistry of his cornet, has made this quote resonate for me."

Dax had cut out that particular quote and kept it in his wallet, long since torn and weathered, yet he continued to read and re-read the quote over the years...the problem was, Dax was no Bix Beiderbecke—but then, no one in the universe was quite as good as Bix, at least that was the consensus of Dax, as well as most of the cornet and trumpet players he'd come into contact with over the years. Dax, was good, very good. But he knew that he didn't have the chops to be compared with the greats, like Miles Davis, Chet Baker, Buddy Bolen, and Bix. He'd paid his dues, and he was a working jazz horn player, but that was it.

The really big-time was not his, was not going to be his, but his love of playing precluded anything else—he had to play the cornet—nothing else in life compared to making the music, and that was his destiny, and he knew it. There was one thing that set Dax apart from most horn players, besides his extraordinary talent—and that was his talent for writing music, both lyrics and the music. He was a one-man show when it came to writing songs—the only problem was that he had never been able to secure a record deal for his songs—oh, there had been several independent and a couple of major labels that had hinted at signing him to a contract, but so far nothing had materialized along those lines. For his final performance at the Blue Moon, Dax planned to introduce a number he'd been working on for the past six months, entitled: A BLUE, BLUE HEART.

He began to sing along to the recorded tape, and it went like this:

LEAD VOCALS:

"We met at the Blue Moon...Our love began, and ended, much too soon...You wore white, I wore black...I need my baby back...Lost in a crazy dream, Trapped in a cosmic moonbeam, Can't believe you're no longer mine, Afraid it's all been wasted time...At the end of love, You're the only cure for my torn...(beat) blue, blue heart...

Dax smiled inwardly, turned off the tape, drew a deep breath, and went to bed. He knew that tomorrow night he'd send his jazz-fans at the Blue Moon home with something to remember.

CHAPTER 23

SATURDAY NIGHT—11 PM—BLUE MOON BAR, BROOKLYN

The place was alive and the music was jiving. The jazz quintet, IN A MIST, led by Dax Bolton, was in a groove. Brooklyn boasts of 90 different ethnic groups within its borders, over 30,000 businesses, some 1,500 churches, synagogues, and mosques, and the Blue Moon was located in Brooklyn Heights, near Orange Street, smack in the midst of that metropolis.

The musicians were playing an old standard, "Theme for Freddy," a Chet Baker recording back in the 60s which got a lot of air-play, and became a standard across the country, after first causing a sensation in jazz circles in southern California. Dax picked up his cornet and tore into a red-hot solo—the crowd was in awe at the beauty of his playing. Out of the blue, a female vocalist joined the players on stage. It was Dax's surprise guest vocalist, Lulu Fontaine, just arrived in the Big Apple from Paris. Lulu was not well known in America, but in European jazz circles, she had gained an instant notoriety as a 'diva' of jazz. She belted out the refrain from 'Arborway' a 1980s standard on which Chet Baker had sung duets with none other than Astrud Gilberto, the singer of the international classic, "Girl from Ipenema.' Lulu's voice was silky smooth—Dax would never be the vocalist that Chet Baker was, and he certainly didn't have the vocal chops to equal Lulu, but Dax backed her vocals as best he could, and the crowd went wild during the set.

As soon as the duet ended, Dax told his audience that he was going to perform an original piece he'd just written and hoped to have recorded soon, A BLUE, BLUE HEART. "And, guys and gals, the really good news is that Lulu will do the lead vocals, and you'll only have to put up with my vocals on the chorus...okay, here we go..."

Lulu shimmered seductively to the mike, smiled at Dax, flirted with the customers seated before her and began to sing..."We met at the Blue Moon, our love began, and ended, much too soon...You wore white, I wore black—I need my baby back..."

Dax joined in the chorus with Lulu..."You said we'd never part, I've been your fool from the start, How do I mend a blue, blue heart..." then, out of the blue, Dax brought his fave Courtois cornet up to his lips and sounded the most melancholy, existential music that the Blue Moon customers had most likely ever heard...the notes flared over the crowd, then seemed to dart away into thin air...the chords silver thin, the pitch picture-perfect, like a Michaelangelo painting—perhaps the musical apparition of Mona Lisa... Suddenly, the trance was broken by a manic burst of sound from Dax's cornet—the sound seemed at times to attack the ear...there was magic in the air as Dax began to drag air into the side of his mouth-piece, then force the notes to drift over the crowd, drifting lazily in an aura of Dax's making, drifting higher, then higher still, until it was as if the sound was capable of rising to the stars...Dax was lost for a moment—the music so grand, so intense, he could be touching the stars—he wasn't even human anymore, he was a spirit—a spirit moving across the galaxy, making his way to an unknown universe...

PART TWO

We don't dream to remember,
We dream to forget...

CHAPTER 24

SAN DIEGO, CALIFORNIA—BROOKSHIRE APARTMENTS

Dax woke up screaming. He was drenched in sweat, still reeling from the phone call he'd received around midnight—he grabbed the alarm clock at his elbow, squinted to make out the time...five am. He angrily threw the damn thing across the room—his frown became a smile when the ringing was instantly silenced as the alarm toppled to the floor.

The wake-up call had been from Detective Burk of the NYPD, Precinct 13, Manhattan. Dax's head still ached from too much scotch the night before—he forced himself to mentally re-play the conversation with Lt Burk..."Hello, is this Dax?"

"Yes. Who the hell is this?"

"Detective Burk—NYPD. Sorry to call you so late, but I have some news—it's not good—but I knew you'd want to know—it's regarding the Laura Vallinsky case..."

"Of course! What is it? Bad news?"

"Dax, before I get into what I don't know, let me tell you what I do know. Okay?"

"Sure—whatever...let's have it."

"Well, we just got a wire from Interpol, Lyon, France, the General Secretariat's Office. Interpol has clandestine contacts within the criminal elements in both France and

Russia. Well, one of these contacts has hacked into a hyper-secure main-frame in which we are privy to ultra-secret emails between various rouge operatives from these two countries. I'm going to read a portion of the email message that was intercepted, as follows: "Subject: VALLINSKY, LAURA—daughter of Victor Vallinsky...subject was last seen as she entered Russian territory, approximately thirty days earlier...she was accompanied by three men, all known to be agents of DAV-D, the Russian Mafia, specializing in high-end art theft, and she is apparently the prisoner of these men. As you know, her father, Victor Vallinsky, is a former double-agent, now thought to be working for the German mafia, and he has been under 'house-arrest' in various locations throughout Russia for the several months. Our intelligence tells us that, apparently, the Russians mafia is fighting with the German gangsters...They are, as we know, bitter enemies...apparently the Russians were trying to blackmail Victor Vallinsky into giving them information about what the Germans were up to—their gambit was to use Laura as the bait to get the old man to open up—our sources tell us that Victor must be a tough old-bird, because they haven't been able to break him, even with the knowledge that his only daughter, Laura Vallinsky, is in their clutches...Apparently the Ruskies tired of the game, and gave orders to execute Laura Vallinsky. There have been absolutely _no_ sightings of her—reports are that she is presumed dead. Until such time as we do get up-dated info, we have to assume that she is, in fact, dead...

"Dax, I told you what I _do_ know...ok?" Detective Burk waited for a response from Dax, hearing none, he went on, "OK, what I _don't_ know, is whether Laura is dead or alive... The bottom line, Dax, is that we just don't know..."

Dax tried to control the toxic mix of anger and confusion inside him which was tearing him apart...Dax struggled to speak, finally muttered, "Thanks for letting me know about the intercepted email...wish it was better news, but like you just said, we really don't know for sure..."

"That's straight-A. Hold that thought, Dax, and hold it tight, because this isn't over—not by a long shot. Believe me, we're going to birddog this thing until we find Laura—one way or the other—we're not going to give up on Laura Vallinsky, and I know that you feel the same way, Dax."

"Burk—"

"Yeah?"

"Nothing...well, I was just going to say that I appreciate you staying with this—for a German citizen who was only in New York on a work visa with the Lyric Theatre...you guys sometimes give the impression you don't care...but, I'm sure that's not always true..."

"Well, I knew you would want to know—for better or worse...as soon as we got any word at all..."

"Detective, you are righteous about that—thanks!"

"Oh, Dax, almost forgot—the Interpol officials released Victor Vallinsky, some time ago, to his own recognizance—big mistake! We've learned that the Russian Mafia found him and have evidently taken him to Kaliningrad, not a good place to be...one of the most dangerous cities in all of Russia, according to my sources. Bottom line—if they've got him, they're most likely using Laura to get information from him...it's a high-stakes game of life and death, at least for one of them. My guess is that it's not safe for Laura, or Victor Vallinsky..."

"Go back to sleep, Dax, if you can, we'll be in touch—good night."

Somehow, Dax managed to drift, fitfully, into a restless slumber, then he began to dream...Dax saw Laura standing alone, at the bottom of a dark pit...he could see the whites of her eyes, glistening in the dark...he woke up screaming...

CHAPTER 25

Dax strolled into his new place of employment, the most-happening jazz venue in southern California, and he was late for a meeting with his friend, Roscoe Bonamasso, "Hey, Roscoe! What's up, brother?" Dax sang out.

"I was beginning to think you were going to stand me up, Dax—where the hell you been?" Roscoe asked, his voice friendly but the under-current of an angry vibe was unmistakeable..."Sorry about that, man. Couldn't be helped—I'll get into it later—it's a little heavy, and it concerns my girl, Laura...

Roscoe let out a loud guffaw..."Aw, hell, Dax, no biggie—I know you're a late-starter—but you always finish in a big way—just the way you make love to those two cornets...still got the magic touch?"

"Well, I don't think I've slacked off too much...yeah, it's still there, folks tell me. You know I love playing jazz, in particular, cool jazz, more than life itself..."

"Yeah, I know—and it's almost killed you a couple of times...am I right?"

"You are righteous—as always...thanks, Roscoe, I mean it. Now, about our show tonight...

CHAPTER 26

Dax had been waiting at the train station for two hours—he hadn't been able to wait until the noon arrival—ever since he'd heard Greta's voice on his cell phone the day before, he'd been too restless to work or to sleep. Suddenly, as the twelve o'clock whistle blew, the train pulled into the station. Greta stepped off the train, her visage shrouded in a sudden burst of sunlight. Greta appeared to be cold—even in the light's embrace. The light reflected off Greta's face, off her hair, off her being—with a hint of wonder. It seemed to Dax that California's light sheen isolated her face with an angelic gaze. A gaze capable of expressing her long and secret innermost thoughts and dreams. Greta shivered with anticipation as she screened the people lined up to greet the passengers. She shot a glance in the direction of Dax, who materialized, seemingly out of nowhere. His gaze was now fixed upon her. As Greta approached Dax, she knew there would be no turning back...

Dax grabbed Greta's bag and flagged a taxi for the drive back to his apartment. Greta had been quiet since she stepped off the train—finally breaking her silence to tell Dax that she was taking a desperate chance to help both Dax and Laura...

"Dax, I know you may, or may not, believe what I have to tell you, but, it is the truth. I haven't been on the up-and-up with you, until now...but, I could not live with myself if I kept you in the dark any longer. I'll tell you more when we get to your place. Okay?"

"Sure—you got it. Whatever the news is that you have, I'm grateful that you've come to me with the information. Did you have any trouble finding me?"

"No. Your pals at the Blue Moon were very helpful in that regard."

"Good—do you have news about Laura?"

Greta motioned for Dax to 'cool it' until they could talk privately, and pointed to the cab driver, then whispered, 'shhh...

Dax knew that he would have to wait until they were in his apartment to find out what Greta had to say...

CHAPTER 27

Greta and Dax breezed into Dax's apartment as Dax opened the door and carried her bags inside. "Make yourself comfortable, Greta. You're welcome to stay as long as you need a place in San Diego. Would you like a drink before we get started..."

"Of course—scotch, no ice, would be wonderful. I'm parched."

Dax quickly poured his finest single-malt scotch, the "Isle of Jura," into a glass for his visitor. "Sure you don't want any ice, Greta," asked Dax.

"Oh, no thanks—I like it just the way it tastes fresh out of the bottle. An acquired taste, I guess you'd say..."

Dax rushed over to Greta and placed the scotch in her hands, and said, "You've got good taste in your scotch, <u>Isle of Jura</u> is a quality scotch—one of the best money can buy," Dax said as he joined his guest on the divan. "Say, before you get into your news, let me ask you a question—okay?"

"Sure—what is it you want to know?"

"Well, it has to do with that New York Detective, Lieutenant Burk...what's your take on him? I mean, do you think he's on the level, or is he covering up for someone—

Greta interrupted: "He's covering up for the entire NYPD, the U.S. Marshals, and heaven knows who in hell else—maybe even hiding some news from Interpol—take your pick, but I tell you, something stinks, and I'm mad as hell about it, I'll tell you that..."

"I think you're right, except—

"Except <u>what</u>, exactly?"

Dax hesitated for a micro-second, cleared his throat, and said, "Except that Lieutenant Burk has been really good about keeping me 'in the loop,' so to speak..."

"And that's good enough for you—enough for you to go on with your life—go on as if Laura never existed, as if she was just a figment of your imagination—a figment of <u>all</u> our imaginations—

"Greta! That's simply not true. You know that Laura and I are in love—I know we had only known each other for a short time, but believe me, every moment of that short time I carry with me in my mind and in my heart—and I carry it with me every step I take..."

Greta jumped off the divan and began to pace back and forth in Dax's apartment as she attempted to begin her story once more..."Dax, I'm sorry if I hit a nerve with my big mouth. I didn't mean to upset you. May I start over? What I have to say is important, and it is information that I have NOT confided to the NYPD or, for that matter, to <u>anyone</u> else...

Dax stood up and reached for Greta's hand—he gently led her back to the divan and gestured for her to be seated. Greta hesitated for a few seconds, finally dropped onto the sofa, picked up her scotch, took a long swallow, wiped her lips, and began anew..."Okay, here we go again. Are you ready for a little reality spinkled in with what you <u>thought</u> you knew—up to this point in time?"

"Of course. Let' s have it—please!"

Greta retrieved a napkin, stabbed daintily at her chin to catch a sliver of single-malt scotch that had escaped her mouth, and began her story..."Okay, here's what I know—

I'm not going to hold back anything—are you sure you're up for this?"

"As sure as I'll ever be," replied Dax.

"Right. The first thing you need to know is that Laura may no longer be in Europe—

"WHAT? How can that be?" asked Dax, his face suddenly a whiter shade of pale than it had been when they sat down, only moments before...

"Laura is lost—what I mean is that my 'contacts,' so to speak, do <u>not</u> know where she is—all they know is that she has been shifted, from place-to place, at least one dozen times since she disappeared from New Jersey. Of course, we know that she was flown to Europe out of JFK. What you may <u>not</u> know, is that connected gangsters, those who specialize, almost exclusively, in the theft and re-sale of master-work art pieces—they, along with a short list of usual suspects, specialize in thefts similar to a major, still unsolved, theft in Boston over twenty years ago. A Vermeer worth multi-millions is still missing, along with several other highly-valued pieces of art from European masters of the sixteenth and seventeenth centuries..."

Dax interrupted again, "What has this to do with Laura? How in the hell can she have anything to do with all this?"

"Dax, calm yourself, please. You already know the story of her father, and the theory that her disappearance is connected to her father—the spin being that she was to be held hostage until such time as her father could be coerced into working with the art thieves. Well, that story has another twist as well..."

"Tell me, please—what's the twist?"

"The old man—that is, her father, Victor, is dead." "Well, hell, that's news! When, and, by the way, <u>how </u>did you find this out?" pleaded Dax. He stood up, his face suddenly ashen and growing, ever more pale, as the seconds slipped away...

"Dax, Sit down, please. I shouldn't have dropped this on you without more foreshadowing, so to speak...I'm going to confess that I haven't been entirely on the 'up-and-up,' so to speak, with you in regard to Laura and her father, Victor..."

Dax wanted to strangle Greta—this 'stranger' who had just casually announced to him that she knew <u>much </u>more about Laura's disappearance than she had let on. He controlled the urge to shout out his questions to Greta, and forced himself to speak in a neutral tone..."Okay, let's have it, sweetheart...from the top, so I don't get lost," Dax growled. "That okay with you?"

"Of course, it's okay, Dax. Hold on to your hat, and please let me finish what I have to say before you ask any questions—any questions at all. Okay?"

Dax cleared his throat loudly, looked away, then forced himself to turn and face Greta once more, only this time his face had hardened, it looked to Greta as though his face was etched in granite, in lieu of flesh and blood..."All right, but I can't promise that I won't have a question or two before you finish your story," replied Dax.

Greta shifted on the divan, tugged at the hem of her skirt and looked Dax in the eye..."Dax, the first thing I need to tell you is just this: I'm not whom I've pretended to be...

"Go on—I figured that from the start," Dax growled.

"You agreed—no interruptions—<u>please!</u>"

Dax nodded his agreement and motioned for Greta to continue anew..."As I was saying," Greta's voice rose an octave as she stood up and began pacing about the room as she spoke..."Okay, Dax, here it is—the 'nitty-gritty.' I'm working under-cover for Interpol. The bad guys don't know who I am. They think I'm a dancer they've persuaded to work with them in return for gaining me entrance into the world of dance—and, believe it or not, those guys do have some 'big-time' pull in the arts world. Anyway, the point is, yes, I'm a dancer, but that was our ruse to gain my acceptance into the gangster's world—the small circle of crooks engaged in 'international art theft'—one of the smartest, and most dangerous, of any outfit working that side of the street, world-wide. And, this 'outfit' is not simply a bunch of thugs,—these guys and gals are very smart, they are very dangerous, and, most of all, they are totally committed to their cause. They'll do <u>anything</u> they have to do to stay in business, that includes murdering anyone who stands in their way..."

"Wait a second! " Dax muttered as he cleared his throat and jumped to his feet and faced Greta. "You're telling me that the dance is a side-line and that you are actually a police officer—wait, not just a police officer, but you are affiliated with none other than Interpol? Is that true? Sounds like a movie plot, or something you've invented to string me along...well, if this is true, show me something—some I.D., to back up your story..."

Dax's complexion had turned in the past few minutes from a pasty grey to a crimson red, and his voice grew noticeably hoarse.

"As a matter of fact, I <u>do</u> have identification, but it's not something I carry around with me on a whim...I mean, it isn't an ID card I flaunt to cash a check..."

"Well, <u>what</u> is it that will verify what you are telling me?" Dax asked, his voice almost a whisper.

"If you'll give me until tomorrow, I assure you I'll have something which will answer your questions. Okay?" Greta sat down and, her face now breaking into a smile, asked, "How about a refill of that wonderful single-malt scotch?"

CHAPTER 28

Dax was lost—it was as if he had stepped out of one nightmare into another...if not a nightmare, then something other than a rational, structured frame of mind. Now that Greta had appeared, out of the blue, with news that she was working undercover for Interpol...Hard to believe, yet her story could be legit—he just didn't know. Could she have made up a story to string him along? And, if so, why would she go to the trouble—then again, if she is lying about working for Interpol, well...Hell, that's it! The wench is lying through her teeth and is trying to set me up..."But, set me up for what?"

Dax could believe that she was something other than a professional dancer...but an Interpol agent—undercover, at that—it was too big a stretch—too outrageous to believe... or was it? He just didn't know. Wait! She said she'd bring 'proof' to back up her story tomorrow...well, tomorrow was almost here—he glanced at this wrist-watch and noted the time...4:30 in the a.m. Time to grab a little sleep before he could face the new day...

CHAPTER 29

Greta was in fine form. She knew that Dax was not convinced that she was whom she claimed to be...and she knew it would be hard for him to accept that she had lied to him, repeatedly, in New York, about who she was, and about what she knew about Laura.

Well, he'd have to believe her now—now that she had come clean with him...now that she'd laid the cards on the table, so to speak...at least, <u>some</u> of the cards...

Well, in a matter of minutes, he'd have his curiosity satisfied—she fished into her attaché case and retrieved a picturesque white back-ground enameled coin—in the center of the coin was a likeness of a falcon. Laura held the coin in her hand, flipped it over and studied the inscription on the other side, and whispered, to herself, the inscription: "Greta Hammett, Agent of Interpol, # 23321." Slowly, she carefully slid the coin back into a hidden compartment in her attaché case. She rang the bell of Dax's apartment and waited for him to open the door.

Dax heard the knock at his door at the very instant his cell phone rang out...instinctively, he answered the call as he opened the door and saw Greta standing there, a strange smile on her face. "C'mon in," he said as he motioned for his visitor to enter the apartment. Dax cradled the cell phone in one hand while he escorted his visitor to the divan and said, "Greta, please be seated—I'll be with you in a minute—need to take this call..."

Greta nodded her head as she sat down on the divan. Dax barked into the phone, "What did you say? Repeat that, please!" His face an inscrutable mask, Dax's face turned a nasty shade of grey as he listened to the caller. Greta knew that whatever the news was that Dax was getting, it wasn't pleasant...

"Okay. Thanks for letting me know..."

Dax dropped the cell phone onto a chair and dropped down on the divan next to his visitor. He started to say something, changed his mind, and jumped off the divan and marched into the kitchen. "Greta, you up for a drink, or is it too early for you?"

Greta glanced at her watch, noted the time, 2 pm, and replied, "I'd like whatever you're having?"

"Okay—single malt scotch it is..."

"Sounds good—haven't had a drop since yesterday," Greta said, her voice straining as she smiled, trying to impart a positive mood into the proceedings.

"One scotch coming up," Dax said as he made some noise with the glasses and scooped up some ice from the fridge.

He glided up to the divan and handed the glass of scotch to his guest as he casually set his glass on the coffee table.

Greta took a swallow of her scotch, glanced at Dax, saw that he tried to act like nothing was wrong, but he wasn't going to win an Academy Award with his performance—she knew something was wrong. "Dax, can you tell me what that call was about, or is it none of my business?"

"You won't believe this—I don't know what to make of it myself..." "What?" Greta asked, her voice laced with concern.

Dax's face telegraphed his anxiety as he positioned himself on the divan to face his guest. "Hard to believe, but that call was from Roscoe, calling from the jazz club, saying that an attractive young woman, about twenty years old, dropped in, out of the blue, and asked for me. When Roscoe asked her name, the woman wouldn't say, just said she was 'a friend of a friend,' and that's all he could get out of her...oh, almost forgot—she did ask when the band would be playing again, and wanted to make sure that I'd be there as she wanted to meet me—that's it—wouldn't give her name or anything else..."

"Odd," quipped Greta.

"Yeah. Real odd. There was one other thing she said to Roscoe—something that doesn't make sense...

"What is it, Dax?"

Dax rubbed his chin, his face a portrait of a man in anguish, and whispered, "She said that I don't know her; however, she told Roscoe that she and I have a mutual friend—a friend who is in some kind of trouble...that's all she would say, then, she was gone..."

CHAPTER 30

Laura was tired—tired of playing the game. She knew she was near the end of her rope. Her captors were also tired of playing the game. They demonstrated their anger and hostility toward her over and over, day by day, but something had finally happened which signaled a change in the weather, a change in their game-plan...oh, there was no one thing she could point to—no one thing that anyone had said or done...it was just that their casual malaise toward her had changed...she didn't know why, didn't know what it might mean...but there was no doubt in her mind that something had spun out of control,—at least <u>something</u> had happened that changed the way they treated her. Not that they were being 'nice' to her—it wasn't that—not by a long shot...but, nonetheless, there had been a change, but, what <u>was</u> it? She didn't know, yet the guards were no longer beating her, and the interrogations were no longer 24/7, as they had been for the past several months that she had been held captive. Suddenly, a black thought, sharp as a knife, buried itself into her psyche, a thought so vile it brought with it a blinding headache...she finally allowed herself to ask the question: Is Vic still alive, or have they killed him with their 'interrogation methods,' methods she knew from her own experience, could prove to be deadly...

Laura felt like a clairvoyant—so real was the image in her mind-screen that she mentally shouted out to her father,

"Dad, hang on a little longer—don't let them kill you—tell them what they want to know...PLEASE!"

Laura opened her eyes and saw only nothingness—the blackness of the room in which she had been imprisoned the past several months overwhelmed her with a malignant sense of dread.

She didn't have to wait for the guards to tell her that Vic was dead—she knew it—she knew it just as surely as if she had been present when he died...

CHAPTER 31

Morgan knew that she had made a mistake—she should never have gone to the Tropicana West Jazz Club. And, she knew that her mother, Laura Vallinsky, would not approve of her recklessness. Her message from Laura had been crystal clear—she let out a cry of despair as she re-read the email for the hundredth time…"Morgan, sweetie, I'm sending this email from an untraceable email address and not from my laptop…I hope you're well and trust that your studies are still interesting to you…just think, one more year in the university and you'll be a college graduate! Just think of it! The first of my family to make the grade to a university degree…in Montreal, Canada.

I've got to be brief and to the point in this email…I'm leaving tomorrow morning for a meeting in New Jersey—a meeting having to do with Pappy—yes, your grand-father, Vic. He's in major trouble and I've got to do what I can to help him, if I can…I'm meeting with some very dangerous characters, but I've got no choice—it's my only option if I am to be of any help to Vic, and it's a matter of life or death, I'm afraid. This may be the last time I'll be able to contact you for some time…it won't be safe for you if I were to communicate with you if things go bad…again, I have no choice but to try to help Vic, if I can…he's in desperate straits—there's no other way…I assure you of that, my darling girl. One last note—I do have a friend, well, more than a friend—a lover—his name is Dax Bolton—he's a cornet player in a jazz quintet in Brooklyn, NY. If the silence from me goes on too long, you might want to contact Dax—he doesn't know you exist—I didn't want to endanger him by giving him too much information about my family in case the bad-guys decide to sweat him out, so to speak...anyway, you can reach him through the club in Brooklyn—name of his group is 'IN A MIST' and they play at the Blue Moon.

Gotta go—study hard—I'm so proud of you, and Pappy is proud of you as well, xxx,Love and kisses...Mom...

Morgan gently folded the email which she had printed out months earlier and placed it in a hidden compartment in her Coach purse. She knew that, if worse came to worse, so to speak, it could play out that it was actually her good fortune that Vic, or 'Pappy' had used his connections in the underworld to conceal certain birth records of her when she was born, out of wedlock, to seventeen-year-old Laura, in Berlin. Laura was interning with the Berlin Ballet Company at the time, and it was a terribly inconvenient time for a budding ballerina to be 'with child.' Laura had never told anyone who the father was, but Morgan had learned from Vic that her mother's lover was a gypsy—someone who roamed Europe, on the lookout for easy money, wine, women, and song...Laura had fallen for his romantic overtures—she called him her 'magic man,' until such time as she revealed to him the fact that she was pregnant—at that point, her lover, Rubio Serenghetti, vanished. She learned later that he had several alias. Serenghetti was just one of many that he used over two continents...he was an enigma wrapped in a mystery, yet Laura was in love—however, she was no babe in the woods, although she sensed from the depths of her inner-being, that Rubio was born under a wandering star, and he'd never be a father—in the true sense of the word.

Morgan knew that when you are dependent on a mother who is still, in many ways, a child herself, and no father in the picture, it makes for 'growing up fast.' The one constant in her short life, outside of her mom, Laura, was Pappy, ole Vic. He encouraged little Morgan to call him 'Vic,' but she had always preferred 'Pappy' to grandfather—he acted, at first, as if he didn't like it, but she sensed that he was delighted by the moniker, but, for reasons of his own, wouldn't, or couldn't, acknowledge that he secretly liked the sound of Pappy—it became their little 'un-spoken' game...

Morgan had learned from a phone call to the jazz club in Brooklyn that Dax had left New York for San Diego, and the manager had been nice enough to give Morgan the name of the club in San Diego where he was now playing with a jazz group...luckily, she was out of school for the summer, so a trip to California was not out of the question... she needed to do what she could to help her mom, and Pappy, if it wasn't too late already...Well, blood is thicker than water, and she felt like it was her time to do what she could, while she could...school would just have to wait—she knew she'd be back...she'd get that degree, she just knew it—the dream was too important—first to Vic, then to Laura, and now, to Morgan herself...

CHAPTER 32

Dax knew now that it was possible he'd never find Laura, the love of his life, alive. He had known it intuitively, of course, but he had not let himself dwell on that fact. He had banished that kind of thinking from taking hold in his mindset. But, now that Laura had been missing for almost seven months, it was impossible to discount the percentages against her even being alive, much less somehow manage to return to him, safe and sound...

He knew that if he were to be strong enough to keep the faith—to keep going ahead with his life and keep playing that cool jazz music with those twin silver cornets, then maybe, just maybe, things would turn out fine. Dax thought of the Bruce Springsteen song, "Think it's gonna work out fine," as he looked at his wrist-watch, noted that he had a short time to get to the Tropicana West in time to warm up for the set tonight. Dax strolled to the apartment parking garage and eyed his ride, a used, but well maintained and great looking American-made Victory Motorcycle, a 2002 Classic Cruiser model V92C, 1510 cc, dual exhausts—black and silver—a beauty! Dax hoped he had made the right choice in transportation since he hadn't owned a motor vehicle of any kind since his move to New York, almost ten years earlier. The Victory Dealer had made one concession in order to make the sale to Dax—they had to provide dual saddle-bags with sufficient strength to support and protect Dax's prized twin cornets while in transit to perform. Dax was initially worried that perhaps he'd laid-off riding motorcycles too long and thought it might be hard to 'get the hang' of it again—he was glad to discover that it all came back to him as soon as he glided out the show-room door.

He glanced again at his watch, noted that he had exactly one hour before 'show-time' at the Tropicana West.

CHAPTER 33

Dax made it into the Tropicana West, with a few minutes to spare, before it was time for rehearsal, so he decided to quench his thirst with a long-neck Coors Light. The barkeep, Nathan, greeted Dax with a nod as he slid the cold brew toward Dax just as he eased onto a bar stool. "How's it hangin,' Dax?"

"Good—all good...how 'bout you, Nathan?"

"Oh, same as always, I guess. Can't complain. What time you guys cranking it up tonite on the main stage?"

"Ten o'clock is the magic hour tonite. Let's see, that gives us exactly one hour to get it down—think we can do it?" Dax replied, the beginning of a smile rippling across his sun-burned face.

"Well, make it rock. Okay?" Nathan asked, his face framed in a half-smile, half-sneer...

Dax didn't know whether he should respond to that particular request, since the Tropicana West was known for 'cool jazz,' so he retorted: "Well, we'll give it our best shot—you know, Nathan, and I'm serious as all hell when I say it, the best music, regardless of the genre, is laced with overtones of other influences..."

"What do you mean, Dax? I really don't get it—I mean, jazz is jazz, rock is rock, blues are blues...

"Not necessarily, my friend—say, I'm dry already—how 'bout another brew?" Dax asked.

"Comin' up, coming up <u>right now!</u>"

"Thanks," Dax quipped as he quickly took a slug of the cold beer, then wiped his mouth and picked up where he left off..."it's like this, Nathan, when you are really into the music, and I mean, REALLY into the music, you're on another wave-length, so to speak—the music tells you where it's going, not the other way around..."

"What? You mean the musician doesn't have control of what he or she is playing? That doesn't make sense—

"What I'm saying is just this...the music knows more than you do—the musician is just the conduit for the magic—

"Magic? What do you mean, exactly, Dax? I don't get it."

"Music can be magical when it's at its best—do you agree with that?"

"Of course, Dax. Music can take you places where nothing else can..."

Dax held up his hands, gesturing wildly in the direction of the stage. "When I'm on that stage, pouring out my heart and soul through the bell of my cornet, what I'm striving for is this: to demonstrate musically that music, and I mean jazz in particular, is a narrative of opposites...light against dark, dissonance against pure intervals of sound, its beginnings sometimes in rapid, swirling patterns, other times like snow in a high wind...and when I'm nearing the end of a piece of music, I want to mesmerize the audience with a shimmering combination of sound of music that accumulates in a glorious sheen, a new dawn of tonality—I want to bend the notes from their natural path to the ear of the listener...when jazz is at its best, when I'm at my best, it's not really me up there on that stage, it's an incarnation of Dax Bolton, an illusion that it's me, but it's actually that old 'magic' I spoke of earlier...when I'm able to achieve what I'm trying to do, the audience will hear an opulent expansion of sound, and hear the division of octaves into more than the usual twelve pitches that you ordinarily hear from the horn. In other words, I'm trying to deliver to the audience an exalted glimpse of a nocturnal paradise of sound—a sound that will linger in the recesses of the mind. When, and if, I can achieve that, I've become a magician. Nathan, does that make any sense at all?"

"WOW!" Nathan shouted as he dropped both hands onto the bar and gazed at Dax. "Man, when you said magic, you meant <u>magic!</u> I get it now. Hey, consider me a jazz fan from here on out—I'm sold!"

Dax let out a laugh and said, "Thanks, Nathan—hope I didn't bore you to death with my monologue—

"Oh, hell, no—just the opposite, man. You hit the nail on the head—music is magic, at least when it's done right. I'm a true believer. Hey, I'll be listening for that magic tonight. Will I hear it?" Nathan asked, a sly smile plastered across his face.

CHAPTER 34

Greta knew something was wrong. She knew it deep in her soul. Who <u>was</u> this girl—this young woman, who had shown up at the Tropicana West asking about Dax? It didn't make sense. And what did she—whomever the hell she was—mean by telling Roscoe that she and Dax were connected in some way to 'someone in trouble? Had Interpol missed something in their research into Laura's background, she wondered...something on the order of a mysterious daughter that no one, including Interpol, knew anything about? Is that even possible? That Interpol could have missed something that important in Laura's background? It didn't seem remotely likely, but she had to make sure—make <u>absolutely</u> certain, that a critical detail such as an unknown daughter was, or was not, a possibility.

Greta had already made inquiries with her contacts at Interpol Headquarters in Lyon, France, but now she was going to contact the USA Interpol Headquarters in Washington, D.C., to conduct an exhaustive search into both Laura Vallinsky's birth records. It would be most interesting to discover at this late date that Laura had in fact given birth to a child; and, if so, how did this information remain hidden from the detailed searches of records conducted by both authorities throughout Europe? Also, <u>who</u> is this love-child, and what is her name, and where the hell does she live—Greta knew of no record of Laura having given birth to a child, much less any evidence that she, or Victor, raised a young girl...

CHAPTER 35

Dax was just finishing a session at the Tropicana West Jazz Club, and he was tired. So tired that when she walked into the club, he thought he was dreaming...the young woman was bathed in a soft crystalline light, a light reminiscent of the fading glow on the screen in a movie theatre at closing time...only this was no movie...<u>who was she</u>? Dax couldn't believe his eyes—the girl met his gaze without missing a beat as she rushed up to the band-stand. Dax stood still—he was incapable of movement of any kind—his brain was on overload—all the circuits had been tripped, it seemed...

"You must be Dax," the young woman said as she stopped at the band-stand and whispered softly, "I'm Morgan. Morgan Fromme. Laura's daughter—I don't think you know anything about me—sorry to surprise you, but I had to meet you." Morgan placed her hands on her hips as the beginnings of a smile rippled across her face.

Dax dropped off the band-stand onto the floor and faced this stranger. He was momentarily at a loss for words as his mind reeled with the information he was desperately trying to process.

Before Dax could reply, Morgan said, "I'm sorry to barge in on you like this, but I didn't know any other way to contact you, and we need to talk—<u>big-time.</u>"

Dax finally gathered his wits and stuttered, "Wow! I didn't know you even existed! Laura never told me about you—

"I know. Is there somewhere we can talk—in private?"

"Of course—we can use Roscoe's office. It's in the back of the club," Dax muttered as he led the way. Morgan continued to smile, although she was not certain what to make of this musician—he seemed a little strange, although she knew that her mom was in love with him. Dax opened a door and ushered his surprise guest into the office. "Before we get started, are you thirsty or hungry? I can get something brought in—

"Well, I could use a Coke—kinda dry just now."

"No problem—hold on a sec." Dax picked up the phone, barked Morgan's request into the speaker, turned back to his guest and said, "it'll be here in a minute or two. Please sit down," Dax pointed to an ottoman in the corner of Roscoe's office and motioned for his guest to be seated.

The bar-keep brought in a Coca-Cola and handed it to Dax's visitor and left. "Okay, shoot, young lady. Wait! Let me say, before you get started, that I assume that you know your mother never said a word to me about your existence...

"Dax, I know that. Laura—I always call her Laura—an old habit, born of necessity, as you will see. Of course, she is my mother and sometimes, rarely, I'll call her 'mummy,' but that's a no-no, although I get away with it now and then as long as I don't over-do it—

Anyway, where was I? Oh, Laura and Pappy, that's my grandfather—otherwise known as Victor Vallinsky, didn't want to acknowledge my existence to the outside world, for a variety of reasons, beginning with the fact that Pappy was involved in, shall we say, 'unsavory' activities throughout Europe. And, these 'activities' involved, among other things, working with the so-called Russian Mafia, as well as—

Dax held up his hands and shouted, "Wait! I know all about Victor's activities, and I can well understand why he would not want his granddaughter to know about his business associates—

Morgan interrupted without saying a word—tears suddenly flooded from both eyes as she tried to regain control of her emotions.

"Morgan, I'm sorry. Please go on...pick up where you left off—please excuse my being rude," Dax pleaded.

Morgan dabbed her eyes with a tissue and said, "Okay—no problem. As I was saying, Vic demanded that Laura's pregnancy with me be done in absolute secret—everything was hidden from public view—he hired the best in the biz to prevent any official records of me being made public. He even arranged for a place for me to be raised, with a 'phantom' family, if you will, in Helsinki, Finland. He arranged for Laura to see me at 'convenient' times, but that was it. It was all done for my 'safety' as well as the safety of Laura. Vic thought it best, and he was the boss—in every way..."

Dax looked at his visitor and suddenly blurted, "Morgan, I've got to tell you something—you're a spitting image of your mother, only a younger version—when I first caught sight of you as you walked into the club, I thought my eyes were deceiving me. My heart skipped a beat for an instant as I thought, for a micro-second, that I was seeing Laura walking into the club—I mean, I knew that couldn't be true, and you are quite a few years younger than Laura—

"I'm exactly seventeen years younger than Laura—that's how old she was when she got pregnant with me...which leads to another reason that Victor wanted my existence kept secret—

"What do you mean? Explain, please!"

"Well, Dax, as you know, mom is quite a dancer—she always has been, and Vic had plans for her—he wanted her to be world-class caliber, and she could have been, too, if—

"IF what, Morgan?" Dax asked, his facial features contorted into painful expressions.

"If Vic's 'associates' hadn't forced Vic's hand into assisting them in some criminal acts which resulted in both Vic and Laura living 'incognito' so to speak, for several years, which made the continuation of formal training impossible at critical times in Laura's training and tutoring by the top talents of Europe. This, of course, tortured Vic because his life-long dream was for Laura to be the dancer that his widow, Mrs Vallinsky, had been in Vienna—Laura had the 'goods,' so to speak, to be world-class, and Vic knew it."

Morgan drew a deep breath, took a swig of her Coca-Cola, and began speaking in a lower octave, her voice a near-whisper as she sprang up from the Ottoman and began walking in circles while she continued her conversation with Dax. "Okay, the last, and perhaps the <u>main</u> reason for Vic and Laura to cling so tightly to the secrecy of my arrival into the world is just this: Vic had felt responsible for the early death of his wife, my grandmother, in Vienna, although none of it was his fault. His grief was shattering—too heavy a cross to bear, and he began to believe that her death was his fault, and his fault alone. Of course, this wasn't true, but, in his mind, he had pushed Mrs Vallinsky too hard, he had pushed her too long—it <u>must</u> be his fault that she had died so young...they were like wild horses—free spirits in the prime of life in old Vienna."

Dax motioned for Morgan to be seated as he poured himself a splash of scotch into a shot-glass and gulped it down. He scooped up a napkin, wiped his lips, set the glass down on Roscoe's desk and smiled at his visitor. "Okay, Miss Morgan—by the way, what is your last name—that is, if you're not going by Vallinsky, which I assume is the case..."

"Fromme. Morgan Fromme—sounds like a pen name, doesn't it? I mean, I don't like it—never have, but that's what I've been stuck with—at least from the time that Pappy, uh, Victor, made the decision that there would be no official record of a female child being born to Laura Vallinsky...

"Okay. Morgan, before we spend too much time on your up-bringing in Finland, please enlighten me on the following topics:

First, are you still in contact with your mother, Laura, and, if so, is she okay? Secondly: Are you still living in Helsinki, or elsewhere? What has Laura told you about me—did she tell you that we're in love? You don't have to answer that last question unless you wish to...

"I don't mind answering any of those questions, but, if you don't mind, I'll start with the last question first: Yes, Laura is in love with you. I'm not certain that she's okay at this point in time—I no longer am in contact with her—she was able to communicate with me, and I don't think anyone else, just prior to her disappearance, and she was afraid that something dreadful was about to happen, but she didn't elaborate...she did say that she would communicate with me when she could, and if she could...oh, in regard to your question about Helsinki, I'm a college student at McGill University in Quebec, Montreal, at this time, although I've taken a 'leave of absence,' so to speak, for the time being... is that about it?"

Dax picked up one of his favorite cornet/trumpet mouthpieces and flipped it over with his right hand, time and again, never taking his eyes off the young lady and replied,

"Let's take a break—get something to eat—then, you can tell me where you live, so that I can give you a lift home—unless you have your own ride?"

"Thanks—I'd like that—took a cab here from my digs. A ride would be appreciated," Morgan said, a wide grin on her face.

"Hope you don't mind a ride on my motorcycle—Victory Special—it'll get you where you want to go even if it only has two wheels...

"No problem—I grew up riding bikes in Helsinki—sounds cool, Dax."

"Good—Let's go!"

CHAPTER 36

Dax and Morgan arrived precisely at eight p.m. at Morgan's digs, the Chateau Orleans Apartments, located on the southern outskirts of San Diego. Morgan hopped off the Victory motorcycle and remarked, "Man, that was a smooth ride—how long you had the bike?"

"Just bought it, couple weeks back. Think it's growing on me...in New York I never had as much as a bicycle, much less an automobile or motorcycle. Didn't really need one in the Big Apple—of course, that meant a lot of cab and subway rides over the past ten years..."

"You were in New York ten years? That's a long time—a very long time to be without a vehicle—how'd you get by that many years without transportation?"

"I just told you—my transportation was mass transit, whether it was by bus, cab, or subway—too many cars in the city, anyway..."

Morgan stopped in front of apartment #22, retrieved her key from her bag, inserted the key and swung the door open as she motioned for Dax to enter. He stepped in and Morgan followed, then flipped on the light switch as she closed the door. "Make yourself comfortable, Dax. Would you like something to drink?"

"Yeah—cold brew would be great!"

"One cold beer coming up—wait, I mean, two cold beers coming up—I'm going to have one with you," Morgan shouted from the kitchenette.

"Sounds good—thanks," Dax shouted as he dropped onto the sofa and stretched his legs. Morgan handed a Coors Light long-neck to Dax as she took a swig from her own brew.

"Thanks again, Morgan. We've got a lot to talk about—a lot of catching up to do. First, let me tell you something—something important that you need to know—okay?"

"Sure. What is it?"

"Are you aware of a lady-friend of Laura's back in New York—a dancer, rehearsing at the same theatre with Laura for an up-coming off-Broadway opening, name of Greta. A tall, blonde German girl—sound familiar to you at all?"

Morgan stared at Dax for a long beat, burrowed her brow, and finally shook her head 'no.' "Can't say that I know anything about her—why?" Morgan's face was stoic, however, her voice betrayed her bravado, and telegraphed the confusion she was desperately trying to hide from her interrogater, Dax Bolton.

Dax studied Morgan for a beat, then replied, "well, turns out that Greta was not exactly whom she said she was—

"What? Explain what you mean-please!"

"I didn't mean to scare you—okay, I'll tell you everything I know—Greta is an officer with INTERPOL, the international police force with offices in 288 countries across the globe. Oh, she's a trained dancer, but she was a plant whose orders were to stay close to Laura—

"Stay close? Why?" Morgan's voice had hardened as her curiosity was now a blend of concern mixed with a sense of dread, or foreboding...

"Stay close to Laura because INTERPOL was aware of the situation with Victor Vallinsky—they knew there was a high-stakes game in the works, in which the Russian Mafia, and some of their cronies, were vying to blackmail Victor into cooperating with them—

"Cooperate with them—why?" Morgan asked, her face lined with worry.

"Okay, let me level with you—this is related to an international investigation into art theft—art theft of 'masterpiece' art-works—irreplaceable pieces which are worth millions of dollars apiece...we're talking thefts that have taken place over the globe, some in the USA, some in various ports of call in Europe, some in Central America—anywhere and everywhere—the criminals involved in this activity are very well organized. Their contacts are apparently 'connected,' if you will, to so-called 'reputable' sources—sources who are willing to pay any amount of money to acquire priceless art—some of these pieces have been missing from twenty to fifty years; hell, in some cases, a few masterpieces of art have been missing for over a century...are you still with me, Morgan? Any questions before I go on? Any at all?" Dax asked, his tone a little less strident than when he began.

"No, I'm good—please keep going—

"Okay, there's something I haven't told you yet—and I need to get to it now...you recall that I just asked you about the dancer in New York rehearsing for a musical—

"Yes, I believe you said her name was Greta—

"Greta Hammett. Anyway, what I <u>didn't</u> tell you is that Greta is here in San Diego."

"She's here <u>now</u>? Why? Is something going on here in California—something that is related to Laura? Is it?"

"Well, it's related to both you and to Laura—of course, now that I know the name with which you've been officially christened...Morgan Fromme...and where you've lived all these years, Helsinki, I've got to pass this on to Greta. Is it okay with you if I ask her to come to your apartment and meet with us—tonight?" Dax asked, his voice now cloaked with concern for Morgan.

"Yes—call her right now and tell her to come over—you've already got my address—she can find me on her GPS if she's not familiar with San Diego...

"Okay—I'll get her on her cell right now—thanks! Hey, before I call, how about another beer?" Dax called out to Morgan. Before he could hit the call button on his I-Phone, Morgan was bringing two Coors Lights into the den.

"That's funny—no answer," Dax said to Morgan after he took a huge swig of the brew. "I left a voice-mail for her—we'll hear back from her soon...in the meantime, tell me about what you're studying in Montreal...

CHAPTER 37

Greta was having a really bad day—not just bad, but bordering on the surreal...the kind of day which makes you wonder why you even got out of bed—she wished now that she had turned off the alarm when the damn thing woke her sharply at six a.m.—she looked at her watch and scratched her head as she noted the time—nine p.m. Had she fallen asleep hours ago? She recalled looking at the time when she dropped with exhaustion into the recliner, and at that time it was about six p.m.—three hours ago... had she been asleep for <u>three</u> hours? Didn't seem possible, but the fact of the matter was that she'd lost three hours, so the inescapable conclusion was that she must have been exhausted—in fact, it had been an unbelievably hard day—first, she'd been chewed out by Interpol, U.S.A. Headquarters in Washington, D.C. Those sons-a-bitches should have known better than to jump on her case—after all, hadn't she done everything by the book? Done it just the way she'd been taught—the way she knew it was supposed to be done? Well, by God, she <u>had</u> done it by the book—not only that, she'd done more than she had to—she was a good officer—one of the 'notable' new officers assigned to the Berlin office of Interpol. Why, she had won 'Officer of the Quarter,' and that meant something—meant that she was playing it by the book—not only that, she knew she'd done good work, had always done good work, and she wasn't going to back down, nosiree, not Greta—not the girl who'd earned her wings, so to speak, among guys and gals with more police work training and experience than she had been privy to...she knew that this job, hunting down the traffickers in theft of world-class 'masterpiece' caliber art works, well, it wasn't plain-vanilla—it was pain-stakeingly hard work—it was not a job in which you punched a clock, turned in a time card, and waited for your pay-check. You worked your butt off, day and night, quite often with no tangible results, with rarely a 'pat on the back' for a job well done—it was work done in solitude, for the most part, work done with little or no recognition, and that was okay with her. What was not okay with Greta was the gratuitous looks and comments she received, mostly from the male-dominated higher-ups in the agency, affectionately known as INTERPOL, the International Police Network, active in 288 countries throughout the world.

And, now that she was working under-cover, first, masquerading for months as a New York dancer, now, working under-cover in California on the biggest case of her career—a 'make-or-break' career-move. She knew she was under the microscope on the 'Vallinsky Affair' as it was un-officially called. And, by God, she was going to make good—make good if it killed her, and, she knew in her heart-of-hearts, sometimes you paid the ultimate price with your life—the price you risk to play the game. From the Bible, we know that even Moses had to pay the price—after forty years of leading his people through the desert to the 'promised land,' he was not allowed to enter in...

A shrill bleep from her cell phone jolted Greta awake—"Hello? Oh, it's you, Dax. Yeah, I can meet you—where?"

What's going on—you'll tell me when I get there? Well, hell, give me about thirty minutes and I'll be there—let me get something to write the address down...okay, shoot...yeah, got it, I'll be there soon—bye!"

CHAPTER 38

Dax heard the knock at the door and he was at the front door before Morgan could get there. He swung the door open, with a flourish, and sounded out a greeting to Greta just as she was poised to knock once more. "C'mon in, Greta—got someone I want you to meet," Dax said as he ushered in their visitor.

Just as Greta stepped into the apartment, Morgan joined Dax and welcomed their visitor with the curt salutation, "Hello—I'm Morgan." Dax watched Greta's reaction—he was surprised that Greta never missed a beat...

"Hello, Morgan—pleased to meet you. I imagine that Dax has filled you in about me. What Dax <u>doesn't</u> know is just this—the agency had informed me, only hours before Dax's call, of your presence in San Diego—my, you've managed to stay out of our sights for a long time, young lady. I'm interested in hearing how you've managed to stay hidden from view, so to speak, all these years...Say, may I trouble you for some liquid refreshment—coffee, tea, whatever? I'm thirsty." Greta made her way to the divan and sat as she awaited her liquid refreshment.

"I'm on it—coffee okay?" asked Morgan as she headed to the kitchenette.

"Sounds great—black—thanks!" remarked Greta.

"Say, Greta, you act like you were expecting me to be here with the mysterious Morgan Vallinsky—that is, Morgan Fromme, it seems" Dax replied.

"Well, funny you bring that up, Dax. Matter of fact, my sources had just alerted me earlier today that Miss Morgan was, in fact, in San Diego—seems she has been in school in Montreal, is it, Morgan?" asked Greta.

"Yes, that is correct. May I call you Greta?" asked Morgan.

"Of course. Please do," Greta said, as Morgan handed her a cup of hot java.

"How did you learn of my existence?" Morgan asked.

"I was just going to ask you the same thing," said Dax, a strange look etched upon his face as he glared at Greta.

"Well, Interpol made deep inquiries into the records that normally are not available to the public. Some of which are available only when funds are offered to certain, shall we say, 'informants.' Those who are found and, shall we say, 'encouraged,' that is—monetarily compensated—for their cooperation with Interpol. Let's say, not only were monies made available, but the offer to 'not prosecute' was part of the bargain. These people live on the edge of the legal system, and, from time to time, 'step across the line.' It is precisely on those occasions that we sometimes elect to not prosecute, but rather 'retain from public view' certain information which can be used as a bargaining chip, if you will, which, in cases like this, pays off big-time. If not for this method of uncovering the facts behind Miss Laura's pregnancy, we'd have never found out anything about Miss Morgan Vallinsky—that is, Miss Morgan Fromme…

Dax and Morgan looked at each other, saying nothing. Finally, Greta broke the stale-mate with the declaration, "Okay, anybody can chime in when they're ready—care to fill me in?"

Two hours later, after Morgan had filled in the blanks for Greta and Dax regarding certain details of her life, and after they had discussed Laura's 'situation,' which, of course, was mostly unknown. Morgan mounted a full-court press—she begged Greta for any information she could possibly provide in regard to whether her mother was still alive, and, if she <u>was</u> still alive, where the hell <u>is</u> she?

"Morgan," Greta began, "if she is still alive, we don't know where she is—please know that we are working 24/7 to find out where that might be. Our people 'on the ground' in Europe think that there is a good chance that Laura <u>is</u> still alive, although it can't be proven at this point in time...the thesis, for now, is that by keeping her alive, they have an 'ace in the hole,' so to speak, in dealing with the players involved...and, that brings me to another part of the equation, a part that, Dax, I've kept from you—until now. Are you ready for that bit of information? Before you reply, let me say, this part of the plan has a role for you to play, and, perhaps a role for Miss Morgan, as well...we'll have to play that one by the ear, for now...if you two aren't too tired, I'll give you a proposed scenario of the plan, and how we intend to carry it out...you guys ready?

Dax and Morgan looked at each other, then nodded in unison, 'yes!'

PART THREE

"Remembering and imagining are, in essence, the same thing."

CHAPTER 39

It was all light and shadow. A trick of the mind. But, somewhere in the hidden region his mind, Dax knew that it was no trick—it was reality. And, reality had tapped him on the shoulder—well, it was <u>more </u>than a tap—it had felt like a crushing slug to the jaw with a sledge-hammer...Dax was back in his apartment—he dropped into his recliner, closed his eyes, and forced himself to re-play the events of the past twenty-four hours, from the moment that Greta had arrived at Morgan's apartment the night before...

Once Greta had been brought up-to-date on Morgan's whereabouts and the origin of her mysterious existence, Dax heard Greta begin to explain Interpol's plan to lead the Interpol police to the traffickers of international art masterpieces, as well as lead to the arrest of the thugs responsible for kidnapping Laura...most importantly, the plan was to rescue Laura—in the event that she was still alive—a point no one can be certain of at this point in time...Dax forced himself to recall bits and pieces of the conversation, and it went something like this...

THE PREVIOUS NIGHT

Greta shot a stern look at both Dax and Morgan, cleared her throat and said "Okay—here's the plan—it could change before it's put into play, but, so you know, and if you agree to cooperate, here's what we plan to do: First of all, guys and gals, I'm going to bring you into an ultra-secret plan—

you can call it 'black ops,' if you like—doesn't matter what you call it, but here it is...the 'agency' that is, Interpol and the FBI, are jointly involved in this project—code name is 'Olympia.' The agency has an under-cover agent called Juan Carlos, who is, to the world at large, the proprietor of an art gallery just outside San Diego.

Juan is, by training, an art critic, recognized as an expert in the art world, not only in America, but in European art circles as well. His job is to get word out, so to speak, to the art 'underworld,' if you will, that he is in the market to purchase some world-class art for some well-heeled buyers, for whom he is the sole agent. The bad guys won't know his real identity, and this could lead us to the criminals who have kidnapped Laura Vallinsky. Any questions?"

Morgan's face was a portrait of agony—she wrung her hands and struggled to ask a question which had tormented her soul. "Greta, do you <u>really</u> think my mother is still alive? That question has been driving me crazy for weeks—is there any chance at all that she's okay?"

"Well, young lady, we don't have documentation that Laura is still alive, but then again, we don't have any evidence that she is no longer alive, so we have to live with our best guess, and that is, frankly, we just don't know... sorry I can't be more specific than that."

"It's okay—that's what I've been telling myself for the past few weeks—in my heart-of-hearts, I feel that she's still alive, even though I haven't heard from her for months..."

Dax interjected, "and that's the way we're going to play it, Morgan. We <u>must</u> believe that there's a good chance that Laura's alive, and by God, we're going to do everything that we can to make damn sure we get her back, alive and well."

Greta smiled and said, "Well put, Dax...now, here's the plan...

CHAPTER 40

Dax knew that if he were going to be able to assist Greta and Juan Carlos in their plan to snag the traffickers operating in the international art theft circle, he'd better become familiar, at least to some degree, with art and the specialty known as 'art criticism.' What he knew of 'art criticism' you could put on the end of a postage stamp. However, his research on Google, as well as a foray into the San Diego Public Library, had illuminated his understanding of both 'art' and 'art criticism.' One of the best rules of thumb was to understand that art criticism is actually a study into the theory of beauty. And, the old cliché, "Beauty is in the eye of the beholder," appeared to ring true with this discipline.

One important point that Dax learned from studying the finer points of art criticism is that the 'secret' to understanding and practicing art criticism is just this: the process of 'thinking,' and the person doing the thinking, are one and the same—it stands to reason that the artist accomplishing the painting, and the painting itself, as well as the <u>process</u> of painting, are, in essence, one and the same...

Dax knew that Juan Carlos had studied at the prestigious Art Students League in New York City, and Carlos had exhibited his works in Cleveland and in Toronto, Canada, a few years ago...

Dax was looking forward to meeting with Juan Carlos—Greta had made an appointment for him to meet with Mr.

Carlos early next week, and Dax was going to be prepared for the meeting, if it took him staying up 'til the wee hours to study the magic of art, and art criticism...

Exactly one week later, Dax walked into the BLUE MATRIX, the art establishment run by Juan Carlos. Dax spotted Carlos the second he entered the art house...Carlos wore a six-button, powder-blue Palm Beach suit, cordovan penny-loafers, pale pink button-down shirt, open at the neck, without the distraction of a tie.

In seconds, Mr Carlos waltzed up to Dax, extended his right hand in greeting, and said, "You must be Dax. Dax Bolton, the cornet maestro..." a dazzling smile on his sun-tanned face.

Dax was momentarily taken off-guard, surprised at the compliment and taken in already by the natural charm of Juan Carlos.

"Well, maybe not a maestro, but I get-by—

"Don't be so bashful, Mr Bolton—

"Dax. Call me Dax, please."

"Dax, it is. What I was saying, although I haven't yet had the pleasure of hearing you play that horn, or horns...I understand you have 'twins,' so to speak...

"Yes, a B(Flat) cornet and an E(Flat) cornet—gives me a little variance in tone and key..."

"That's what I hear—pleased to make your acquaintance, Dax. Why don't you step into my office for our visit, then I can show you around—what do you say?"

"Great—let's do it. Lead the way, Mr Carlos—uh, Juan..."

"Here we are, Dax," muttered Juan Carlos as he closed the door to his office and motioned for Dax to be seated. "I appreciate you taking the time to see me—and my place of business. What do you think of the shop, so far?"

"Looks fantastic, that's for sure. Of course, as I think you already know, I'm not an art guru, by any stretch of the imagination, although I do have a 'thing,' if you will, for beauty—"

"And, beauty is the name of the game—both in the creation of art and for the art critic—are you an art critic, Dax? I mean, I know you're a wonderful musician, but, as you know, art and music are two different animals, if you will—both encased in the art world, so to speak, but different specialties, different talents and different paths, to 'enlightenment,' if you will..."

"Of course, I agree. As I was going to say, I'm not a patron of the arts, so to speak, but, being a musician has vested me with an appreciation with the 'beauty,' if you will, of all the disciplines in the world of art, whether it be painting, writing, acting, music, whatever...

"Well put, Dax. Would you like something to drink before we get into the matter at hand?"

"A bottle of water would be super—thanks!"

Juan Carlos reached into a cooler just inches from his chair, grabbed an OZARKA bottled water, handed it to his visitor, and began, "Here you go, Dax. Now, to the business at hand..."

CHAPTER 41

Dax was in rehearsal for a big show at the Tropicana West on Saturday night. He had learned from Juan Carlos that his part of the plan was marginal—he had only to be available at certain times at the BLUE MOSAIC art house to 'assist' Mr. Carlos when there was a need for some 'off-site' work, the nature of which had not yet been fully explained to Dax. All he knew was that it could be dangerous due to the criminal element they were trying to entice into doing business with Juan Carlos at the BLUE MOSAIC.

He did manage to convince Morgan to 'stay away,' from the premises of the BLUE MOSAIC—for one thing, it was possible that the bad guys were aware of the existence of a 'missing daughter,' and there was no need in spiking any curiosity in the matter of a teen-aged girl who happened to be a splitting image of her mother, Laura Vallinsky. However, Morgan did win one round in the discussion about her role—she would be kept apprised of any development in the caper to ensnare the culprits into the trap laid for them by Interpol and the FBI. Morgan had to content herself with daily up-dates from both Dax and Greta.

Dax was going to do an encore at the Tropicana West of the finale in Brooklyn at the Blue Moon, on his last night before leaving New York. This time, there would be no Lulu Fontaine, the Parisian song-bird who had so overwhelmed the audience at the Blue Moon...so, Dax had to come up with an alternative singer—but, who would it be? The problem was that he just didn't know, and he only had three more days to show-time...

CHAPTER 42

Lulu Fontaine—that's who he needed—Dax knew he had to have a show-stopper for the spectacular show he wanted to put on at the Tropicana West on Saturday night. But, where the hell <u>was</u> she?

He hadn't heard a word from her since their farewell show at the Blue Moon months ago. Lulu had only said, "Dax, I've got a couple of personal irons in the fire—irons that have to be taken care of before I can schedule any future performances—that's all I can tell you right now—okay? No hard feelings?" Lulu asked, her face gave away nothing as she broke the embrace with Dax and walked out of the Blue Moon, and disappeared into night, along the boulevard of broken dreams that reverberate in the dark heart of Brooklyn.

Dax drew a deep breath and tried to recall any casual piece of information that she may have given him as to where she was headed. Nothing—absolutely nothing. He was at a loss as to her whereabouts, and didn't have a clue whom he could find—at this late date—to breathe vocal magic into the show on Saturday night, now only two days away...

THE NEXT DAY

Dax awoke with a headache—his ears were ringing... wait, was it his ears, or was it his cell phone ringing...it took another few seconds before he realized that it <u>was</u> his cell... "Hello, yes, this is Dax—who wants to know?" Dax listened and suddenly realized that the caller was the answer to his prayers..."Is this <u>really</u> you, Lulu? I can't believe it—I have looked, high and low, and couldn't locate anyone who had an idea of where the hell you might be—and, as you will recall, you wouldn't, or couldn't, tell me where you were headed after our gig in Brooklyn...where are you, sugar?"

"Well, you're not going to believe it, but I'm in San Francisco. How you doing in San Diego? Liking it?"

"Yes, I'm liking it—it's not New York, but then, there's only one New York! Right?"

"Of course, you're right. I'm going back to Paris in a few days, but plan to stay in California a little longer—

"Lulu, you are the answer to my prayers...can you get your butt down to San Diego—I need you to help reprise our gig we did together in Brooklyn at the Blue Moon—you up for it? I'll make it worth your while...that is, Roscoe will make it worth your while—he's already given me a green light to hire someone 'really special,' as he put it, and you are the most special singer I know...what do you say—one night—this Saturday—can you do it?"

"Well, since you asked so sweetly, I'll do it! What time do you need me there for rehearsal on Saturday? I've got a flight to Paris Sunday afternoon, from San Francisco, but I can change it to San Diego—okay?"

"You got it, sugar—you truly are the answer to my dreams. I'll send you an email with the directions to the TROPICANA WEST—and let's shoot for rehearsal at noon on Saturday, show time is at ten p.m.—sound good? Oh, almost forgot—you can stay my place Saturday night if you wish."

"You got it—see you Saturday at noon—love ya, Dax!"

"Thanks, Lulu—oh, almost forgot—what is your email address?"

"Yes, would help if you're going to send me directions, wouldn't it? Here you go—

CHAPTER 43

Morgan was restless. She felt like a ship lost at sea, her hopes of seeing her mom, Laura, alive...seemed like a remote possibility. Something, much deeper than what her brain could fathom, was at play in this merry-go-round called life...she wanted to believe that Laura's disappearance would end happily—not unlike a Hollywood movie of yesterday, reflecting a rainbow of light at the end of the dark tunnel. Of course, she'd settle for a 'ray of light' into the darkest regions of her heart and soul—an elixir for the soul.

The possibility that she would never see her mother alive again had begun to take hold of her mind, and she couldn't let it go—at least not completely. Suddenly, a sense of wonder permeated her being—it was as if fields of light, which had been playing hide and seek with her, had thoughts of their own, which suddenly took a front-row-seat to her melancholy...she felt as if she were in a limbo of an unearthly magic—a magic so true, so real, that it just had to be speaking the truth—the truth that Laura <u>was</u> still alive...

Morgan remembered something she had learned at the university in Montreal, just a few months ago—funny that it felt like a life-time ago...she had been studying the concept of time—that is, in the human mind, there are three levels of time, Level One: Life as we see it in public events in the 'real' world; Level Two: Our personal environment; Level Three: Life of the mind; imaginary—life as we want it to be...

CHAPTER 44

Laura Vallinsky knew that something 'big,' was in the offing...it was unmistakeable that <u>something</u> had happened, she just didn't know how this 'change' would affect her. After all those months of being held captive by these criminals, she had been spirited away from her last 'holding station,' which she knew to be somewhere in a Russian province. She let out a sign of relief when she over-heard one of her captors say that he was happy that they were finally heading to the Vendee area of France—an improvement from the boring and grim area they had been stuck in for several months.

Laura knew the Vendee area well, and in fact had traveled in the area about ten years earlier—she knew that it was a favorite vacation area for tourists—in fact, tourism was one of the main industries in the area. They were headed to the town of Challans, not far from the Atlantic Ocean and in the west and central part of France—Laura recalled the Pays-de-la-Loire area as being a beautiful place.

She thought of the irony that her daughter, Morgan, had wanted to go to school there at the Catholic Institute of Higher Studies, just outside the town of La Roche-sur-Yon. Because she and Victor Vallinsky felt that Morgan needed to get away from Europe, they had elected to send Morgan to Montreal for her higher education.

Laura thought back to what she remembered about the Vendee Area...it could be important to her in the event that she can manage an escape from her captors while located in this beautiful area. A thought suddenly took hold of her thought-process, and her mind took off on a trip of its own... suddenly she knew the reason they had shifted from Russia to France. It just <u>had</u> to be because of the Batista Family—residents of the Vendee Area, primo buyers of masterpiece works of art, whether they be in the form of painting, sculpture, drawing, mosaic...wait a second! Mosaic? Yes! That must be the key to this wicked game for which these criminals had singled her out—she knew very little about the business of trafficking in stolen art, and she knew, from conversations with Victor, that several very significant and important mosaics had been stolen over twenty-five years ago, at least. And, this art had never been recovered—this she knew from the little Victor told her. She had always gone out of her way not to interfere into Victor's affairs—this was verboten—plus, she knew that Victor was not proud of the role he had played over many years, working, off and on, with some of these master criminals. Victor had shielded little Laura as best he could, and, of course, had insisted that arrangements be made for little Morgan to be raised in Helsinki, rather than in Berlin with Laura, her birth-mother. Victor had made all the necessary arrangements to place Morgan with an intelligent and attractive woman in Helsinki—Jordis Fromme. Jordis and Victor had been lovers, after the death of Victor's wife in Vienna. Victor had been heart-broken when Jordis left Berlin for Helsinki, but she had made up her mind to forge a new life, and, by God, she did it. She saw, even back then, a bad end for Victor if he did not sever the tentacles of the Russian Mafia, and he had tried, and had tried hard, to do what she wanted, but he just could not bring himself to 'walk away,' from the biz, and, of course, he was 'encouraged' not to leave—often it was couched in no uncertain terms…"Victor, if you leave the 'outfit,' you could end up taking some of us with you, somewhere down the line, and, unfortunately, that's not acceptable—we will not tolerate it, so forget about your 'plans,' as you call them, and accept who you are, and <u>what</u> you are—it's better that way, for all of us, and, Victor, it's much better for you. I hope that we have an understanding—do we have an understanding, Victor?" He'd had to reply, "Yes, we have an understanding."

TWO DAYS LATER

"Laura, do you know why you're here, in France, instead of lying in an unmarked grave in Russia?" asked her tormentor, Mikael Pratt.

"No. Could it be my good looks?" Laura snarled. She didn't bother to look in his direction as she responded, her words laced with anger.

"Well, looks like the lady bears a grudge…and we've gone out of our way to keep you in good spirits, haven't we, my dear?"

Laura did not bother to reply to this comment, and began to work on her dinner, a cold plate of jambon—mogettes (ham and white beans), as she drank from a plastic water bottle. Mikael Pratt continued to stare at his prisoner without further comment. Finally, Laura relented and turned in his direction, folded her hands, as if in absolution, or at least, in an attempt to bridge the icy waters of their relationship of victim/captor.

Finally, Mikael tired of the game, smiled, this time a real smile, and replied, "What the hell, Laura. We're not gonna kill you—at least not yet, don't you know that?"

"Well, I wouldn't have bet the farm I'd be alive at this point in time. I do appreciate you letting me know of the death of my father, even if you and your 'associates' were responsible—guess I should be thankful that you, at least, allowed me to say good-bye to him before the burial—

"That was not my call, Laura—you should know, if I'd had my way, you wouldn't even know about his death—we'd still be using the 'possibility' of his death to strengthen our hold on you—I was out-voted on that one, that time a break fell you way—can't guarantee you'll be getting any breaks from here on out—understand?

"Yes, but I do have a question—with Victor dead, why have you continued to keep me captive—to what end will it serve to keep me here, indefinitely?"

"I can't answer that, sweet thing—not my call. However, I will say this: there are very explicit plans which involve you, and that means we need you alive—for now. That doesn't mean you won't become 'expendable,' once you are no longer useful to us. Any more questions?"

"Yeah, can I have some wine?"

Mikael laughed and marched out the door, slammed the metal door shut, threw the deadbolt into place. Laura sighed, turned on a small TV on which she could see only DVD movies—she was allowed no news updates, no newspapers—nothing at all. Laura now understood what philosophers, writers, and artists meant by the term, 'existential.' Her persona was existential, she had become a non-person, a non-entity, awash in nothingness.

CHAPTER 45

Greta was worried. She had reason to worry. She clicked off her cell phone and looked at Dax. "Bad news, Greta?"

"Well, it's not good—then again, it could be nothing, but I have a bad feeling that something has gone wrong—

"Wrong? Hell, what did Juan have to say?" Dax pleaded—the wild look in his eyes telegraphed his worry...

"Well, I'm glad we're here in your place instead of at the Blue Mosaic, with Juan—he's a mess!"

"What do you mean—a mess? What gives, Greta?"

"Okay—say, pour both of us one of your wonderful, trademark, single-malt scotches—please?"

"You got it—give me a minute or two and they will be ready in a jiffy—neat or ice?"

"Better make it neat, this time, Dax."

Dax handed a glass of his best scotch, neat, to his guest, as he dropped a couple of ice cubes into his glass, and took a large gulp of the whiskey, never taking his eyes off the normally unshakeable Interpol Agent, Greta Hammett. He had never seen her quite as animated, or quite as nervous, as she was at this moment.

"Okay, Dax, here's the scoop from Juan—it may not be a fatal problem, but if it's got any legs at all, it will mean that our plan may not work—

"Why not? Are they on to Juan?

"Well, his European contact left a caustic message on Juan's cell...

"What did it say?" Dax asked, taking care not to over-step his place in this charade...he knew that he was on shaky ground, as it was, dealing with top-secret, international criminal activity, and here he was—a horn player in a jazz septet at the Tropicana West, trying to play like a detective, caught between (1) some dangerous gangsters in Europe, (2) Interpol, (3) FBI, and (4) Brooklyn N.Y.P.D., in the form of Lt Burk, whom touches base, from time to time, with Dax, although it's been at least one month since he's had a report from Lt Burk. Dax is not at liberty to reveal to Burk the fact that Laura's daughter, Morgan, has shown up in San Diego—this is top-secret information that has got to be held 'tight.' Dax wonders, from time to time, why Burk is still taking the time to call him, but is glad that the detective is still interested—maybe he felt guilty over his treatment of Dax when he first reported Laura missing...Dax didn't know, but a nagging 'sixth sense,' or something like it, had taken hold of Dax, a feeling he could not explain, could not understand, a feeling that, maybe, just maybe, Lt Burk had another agenda...but, if that's true, and the odds are that there's nothing to it, <u>why</u> would Burk continue to call Dax since the Brooklyn NYPD had been called off of the case by the FBI? He didn't know the answer to that question...

Greta stared at Dax for a long beat, and asked, finally, "Dax, are you okay? You seemed to be in another world, or in a trance..."

"Oh, sorry, Greta—just had a thought about Lt Burk of the Brooklyn NYPD—you know, he still calls me, from time to time, in regard to Laura, but never has any news...I wonder why he's still on the case..."

Greta gave Dax a stern look and replied, "That <u>is</u> weird, Dax, unless he just feels he owes you...still it's odd...in fact, I can tell you that the NYPD is officially 'off' the case—between the Washington Bureau of Interpol, and the home office in Lyon, France, as well as the FBI, it's out of his hands...that is strange...I just don't know—maybe he's a little 'too' anxious to keep you posted...

"Greta, you don't think he's trying to 'shake' me down, so to speak—what I mean is, maybe he's trying to find out what I do know...does that make any sense?"

Greta cast a long stare at Dax, poured herself another shot of scotch, pausing momentarily to vigorously drain the glass. She placed the empty glass back onto the coffee table, looked up at Dax and said, "You don't think he's got some kind of 'secret agenda' in regard to Laura?"

"Nah—too big a stretch—but, still, that 'sixth-sense' of mine won't shut up—I'm about 99% sure that it's my imagination—I mean, what ulterior motive could Burk have? I can't think of one," Dax said as he poured another round of drinks.

Greta smiled and thanked Dax for the refill, sat back, and asked, "Are you ready for the news from Juan Carlos? It's not good, and if it's true, it means that the game will be over in San Diego soon. We'll be heading for a new destination—a locale outside the USA—but, as you know, Interpol goes anywhere, and everywhere...

"Greta, before you get into the call from Juan, does this new info have anything to do with Laura? Any news of her?" Dax asked, the tone of his voice wavering with the emotion he had tried so valiantly to control.

"Dax, here's all I know...Juan's contact told him that 'something had changed,' apparently, his 'seller' was no longer interested in making a sale to Juan—the contact would only say that they had an offer they couldn't pass up, and would only say that the new buyer was of 'no importance' to Juan—in other words, he wouldn't disclose, either the identity of the supposed 'buyer,' or where the sale would take place...

"So, where does that leave us, if this is true?"

"Don't give up too soon, Dax. My experience is that this may be a 'trial balloon,' so to speak. Often, the bad-guys will float an alternative, for various reasons, one of which is to gauge the reaction of a potential buyer—if someone reacts too strongly, the contact assumes that price is no object—so, they'll back off, then jack up the price to an astronomical amount—this could all be just a ploy—

"You mean my studying up on art, and the fine points of art criticism, and art appreciation, was all wasted time?" Dax said, his voice faltering between a forced laugh and a bitter tone. "Greta, I've got to find out the truth about Laura—its killing me, not knowing whether she's even alive..."

"I know, Dax. Listen, you know none of us will rest until Laura is safely back, and, if she is still alive, and I think she is, we'll find her—you've got my word on that."

Dax leaned across the divan and hugged Greta as he brushed back a tear from his eye, and said, "I know it, Greta—I know it just as surely as we're sitting here...I sleep a little better at night, knowing that you, Interpol, and the FBI are on the hunt—I'll do what I can to make it happen, as well...

Greta bid Dax a farewell as she walked to the door of Dax's apartment, turned and asked, "Say, let's talk for a minute about something else...when did you say you're having the big show at the Tropicana West?"

"Saturday night, at ten p.m.—be there a little early and I'll introduce you to my 'surprise vocalist', Miss Lulu Fontaine."

"Oh, I'll be there—you can count on it—good night, Dax, I'm outta here."

"Yeah, I'm hitting the sack soon myself—so long, detective," Dax shouted as Greta waltzed out the front door.

CHAPTER 46

It was just eight hours until 'show-time,' and Lulu was nowhere in sight. However, Dax wasn't worried—he knew that if she'd encountered any problem, any problem at all, she'd have called...still, he couldn't really relax until she walked through the door of the Tropicana West in the heart of San Diego. Dax took one more look at his Lucian Picard wrist-watch...five minutes after two p.m. Dax thought to himself, well, she's only two hours late, could be worse... of course he couldn't imagine what could be worse—all the flyers had been handed out, announcing their 'surprise vocalist,' an International star in the world of cabaret...from Paris, no less...yet, where the hell was she?

"Hello, Dax! Been missing me, sugar-pie?"

Dax never missed a beat as he spun around, grabbed Lulu Fontaine and wrapped her in a bear-hug. "Baby-Doll, where have you been? Are you all right—been wondering if you were okay?"

"I'm good, Dax. Sorry I didn't call—damn battery on my cell died and I couldn't get to a phone—sorry about that—the cab just dropped me off couple minutes ago—I got here as fast I could—plane was off-schedule, then, too much traffic at the air terminal—you know how crazy and stressful flying can be these days...

"You said it, Lulu. No sweat—just glad you're here, and, I hope, rarin' to go," Dax said, his face breaking into the largest smile to cross his face since the day Laura disappeared from his life.

"Lulu, would you like a bite to eat, and a chance to 'freshen up,' a bit, before we hit the boards?"

"That would be great, Dax. Been a long time since our gig in Brooklyn—did we give 'em a show, or what, that night?"

"Baby, you were magic that night—I still hear from some of the guys back there and they're still asking me...when is Lulu coming back—with, or without you, Dax—no hard feelings, but, hell, we only got to play with her once, and we'd love to do it all over again. They're going to be upset that you're here, and not on the stage at the Blue Moon, doncha know?"

Lulu laughed as she set down her bags and asked, "Which way to the ladies room? I've got to get freshened up before I dig into some food—

"Straight ahead, Lulu—you can't miss it," Dax said as he worked to supress a laugh. "Take your time—the rest of our septet won't be here until about nine...that way, you and I can jam a little bit on our own—all right by you?"

Lulu shouted over her shoulder as she made tracks to the ladies room, "Sure thing—whatever you say...

CHAPTER 47

Dax thought it was time to spring his 'surprise' on Lulu—he had decided the night before that he wanted to add some material he'd been working on for the past two months...a sprinkling of tunes from the 1942 musical, "For Me and My Gal," by Busby Berkeley—the Broadway hit had been a kaleidoscopic production on the stage, and later made into a Hollywood film, starring Judy Garland, in her first grownup role, plus Gene Kelly, in his first movie role ever—a story set in the late nineteen-teens vaudeville, based on the song-and-dance team of Jo Hayden and Harry Palmer, whose career and romance were interrupted by World War I. It's a patriotic work that relies strongly on blues-drenched harmonies of ragtime-era songs. Plus, Dax knew that the film was a favorite of Lulu's, due primarily to the presence of Gene Kelly, her all-time favorite Hollywood dancer/actor/singer. She had told Dax often that she'd seen the film at least twenty or more times...not to mention the number of performances she'd seen Gene Kelly singing and dancing, "Singing in the Rain," in the classic movie of 1952, also starring Leslie Caron, "An American in Paris."

Dax knew that Lulu would love the music, and might even be persuaded to sing along with the music—he knew she would be comfortable with joining in on the performance...

"Oh, Lulu, you're back—ready to practice our numbers from the Blue Moon gig, back in Brooklyn?"

"Hell yes, let's get it on," Lulu answered, a huge grin on her face. "Let's do it!"

ONE HOUR LATER

"Whew! That was a workout, Dax."

"You said it, Lulu. By the way, you're in even better voice, if that's possible, than when I last heard you in Brooklyn... wonderful, just great—really glad you decided to join in on the fun tonite. By the way, got a special surprise I haven't told you about...are you ready for this—"

"I'm as ready as I'll ever be—what's up?" Lulu asked.

Dax outlined the "For Me and My Gal," act, and Lulu lost her composure—"Would I be willing to join in? Of course I would—you know, Dax, that's one of my all-time favorite musicals...I really don't need rehearsal to join in on the vocals...of course, I'm too rusty to do any dancing, but would love to harmonize with you on the vocals."

"Great! That's what I wanted to hear. Okay, we've got a little time before we 'hit the boards,' so you might take a little breather, get refreshed, whatever, and remember, showtime is ten p.m sharp. Okay?"

"You got it, Dax. I'll be ready." Lulu said as she headed toward her dressing room.

CHAPTER 48

The Tropicana West was over-flowing—the venue normally could accommodate eighty or ninety customers comfortably, but tonight's crowd numbered over one hundred. A few folks were clustered into a more intimate setting than what they were accustomed to, but that hadn't caused any problem to the bartenders and wait-staff at the jazz club—everyone knew this was a special night and, by God, no one wanted to be responsible for an unhappy customer, 100% of whom were jazz enthusiasts and all were 'hyped-up' over news of Lulu Fontaine's appearance. The West Coast jazz fans are one-of-a-kind, and they appreciate good jazz the way other folks might enjoy an NFL Super Bowl game...

Dax, Roscoe, and the other members of their septet were all accounted for, being a total of seven musicians, and, of course, that special guest from Paris, France, Lulu Fontaine. Dax and Roscoe took care of the cornets, while the two saxophonists were Bruno Levinsky, and Tigy Winer. On piano, they featured none other than Charlie Moon— while Harold Blomquist was featured on violin. Completing the septet on guitar was Lionel—the man with no last name.

At precisely ten o'clock, the musicians took the stage and began warming up for the show. Within minutes, all were good-to-go; without further ado, Dax and Roscoe stood front-and-center, inserted mouth-pieces into their cornets, and blasted into the Tropicana West intro number, 'Wild Bird.' The other musicians sat silently, watched this duo perform for the sell-out house. The tempo of the music was reminiscent of 'cool jazz,' although the finer points of the music pointed to 'free jazz,' which, while differing from 'cool jazz,' free jazz shared attributes of both. Their intro set the tempo for the rest of the show.

Lulu watched and listened, just off the stage, and it seemed to her that Dax sounded even better than he had in Brooklyn. It appeared to Lulu that a contest between Roscoe and Dax was in the works—a contest to determine which cornetist was the maestro...At first, Dax jettisoned a journey of opposites—setting first, light—then darkness, dissonance against pure intervals...beginning in rapid, swelling patterns, like snow in a high wind, thought Lulu. She knew that Roscoe was not going to go down without a fight as she listened to his cornet blend notes from their 'natural' paths out of his horn—his horn emitted an opulent expanse of sound at the same time that the music flowed seamlessly from the bell of the instrument.

Lulu remembered a comment she had heard from one of the jazz fans at the Blue Moon in Brooklyn, on the night she had shared the stage with Dax—the fan had whispered to a pal, while listening to Dax play, that 'this music is a glimpse of a nocturnal paradise of sound—a sound that lingers in the recesses of the mind..."

Lulu shook off her reverie and steeled herself to be ready to perform—her spin in the spotlight was seconds away...

Roscoe grabbed the mike and announced, "Ladies and Gentlemen, it gives me great pleasure to introduce our featured vocalist of the night, Miss Lulu Fontaine, direct, from Paris, France—please give her a San Diego welcome!"

Lulu took the stage as the audience clapped furiously. Dax gave her a bear hug, Roscoe bowed in her direction and the jazzmen sprang into a jazz anthem, "Let's Get Lost," while the jazz septet lent their music to her vocals. She quickly covered a couple of other favorites, then paused to catch her breath as someone in the audience shouted, "Please do "A Blue, Blue, Heart." Lulu smiled at her interlocter, turned to face Dax, and said, "That's what I'm here for—here you go..."

Dax thought for a moment that he and Lulu were back in Brooklyn, on his last night at the Blue Moon, when he had introduced the song to the world at large—surprised that word-of-mouth had spread to the west coast. He had purposely not performed it since the Blue Moon, mainly because he didn't have Lulu for the vocals, and secondly, because he was too caught up in the matter of Laura Vallinsky—he had put it in the back of his mind, until such time as Laura was back, safe and sound, and into his life again...it took just a few moments for him to segue back into the here-and-now. He faced the musicians, made sure everyone was 'good to go,' glanced one last time at Lulu, she winked back at him, and Lulu began her vocals, giving Dax a few moments to infuse his cornet into the proceedings, the rest of the musicians blended into the melancholy tune...

Just as in Brooklyn, it was déjà vu all over again—the audience loved the song. As the music ended and Lulu finished the last lines of the chorus, a roar of clapping burst forth and spread throughout the Tropicana West. "A Blue, Blue, Heart" was a knockout punch.

Without further ado, the septet launched into Dax's surprise—the music of Busby Berkeley from "For Me and My Gal,"...the audience loved the music—most were familiar with the Hollywood classic and stage musical from many years before.

At two a.m., most of the customers, jazz fans all, were still at their tables, tired but exalted by the music they had just experienced. Everyone, with one exception, seemed to be in great spirits—that one person was Dax Bolton—he had noted, much earlier, that Greta had not shown up for the show, as she had told him she would. Dax knew that Greta had been <u>really</u> looking forward to the event. He also knew that she wouldn't have missed it—if she had any choice. He hoped, with all his heart, that her absence was not a harbinger of bad news...his thoughts turned instantly to Laura...

PART FOUR

"Memory is a flicker between the past and the present; it is the eternal house where we hold each other forever..."

Andrew Miller 'The Marriage Artist'

CHAPTER 49

Greta was in a funk...first, she had just been told by Interpol Headquarters in Lyon, France, that the caper originally planned to take place in the San Diego area, specifically at the BLUE MATRIX art house, code name: OLYMPIA, was not going to happen. She learned that Interpol had intercepted (hacked) into confidential emails between the traffickers in international art theft masterpieces who had kidnapped, and held, Laura Vallinsky for the past seven months.

Greta was surprised to learn that, number one, Laura had been prisoner in the area of Vendee, France, her captors having left their hideout somewhere in the former USSR, weeks earlier; secondly, she now knew that the bad guys were planning to leave, Laura in tow, for an undisclosed location in Mexico. Interpol knew only this—the buy would take place in the vicinity of Mexico City. She was heartened to learn that Laura was still alive. Now that she'd had time to mentally process this information, and come to terms with it, she began to feel a tinge of hopeful anticipation—she would now have to gear-up for a trip to Mexico. But, what about Dax and Morgan? What was she going to tell them? Greta knew that it would not be possible to tell them—it would be too dangerous—and, of course, they could not be permitted to accompany her in the pursuit of the criminals. Much too dangerous for amateurs...Of course, she'd let them know that Laura <u>was</u> alive, and, hopefully, doing well...

She'd tell them that the 'game' was over in San Diego, the sting would have to play out elsewhere. There was no need to tell them more than that...that's the way it would have to be.

There was nothing in the world Greta could do to change a thing. Still, one question had lodged in her mind, and she couldn't answer it—<u>why</u> was Laura still alive, and why were they bringing her with them to Mexico? She knew that Victor had died, so there was no reason for the criminals to keep her alive—unless she was the missing key to a puzzle she hadn't figured out. What could it be? She didn't know, but she knew, in her heart-of-hearts, she'd have to figure it out, and the sooner the better...

CHAPTER 50

Dax and Morgan had been waiting for six hours, and there was still no word from Greta. Dax had treated the teen to a steak dinner at Maggiano's, a Five-Star Italian restaurant, only minutes from Morgan's apartment. After dinner they headed to Dax's apartment for a meeting with Greta. The meeting time was to be seven p.m—Dax glanced for the umpteenth time, and noted, that it was now nearly nine o'clock. He had never known Greta to be late for anything—much less on the occasion of their last meeting with the Interpol Inspector before she was scheduled to depart San Diego for an unknown destination. He knew why they were not invited—wherever it might be, it was too dangerous an undertaking for the teen daughter of Laura. And, of course, Dax was no Sam Spade…hell, he was a horn player, a pretty damn good one—still, he was not a trained police officer, and certainly no 'hot-shot' detective.

It was near midnight when Greta showed up at Dax's apartment. The buzz of the doorbell awoke Morgan from a sound sleep on Dax's divan. "I'm sorry!" shouted Greta as she waltzed into the apartment. "Totally my fault—should have called and let you both know that I was tied up—couldn't be helped," the Interpol detective said as she eased onto the divan next to Morgan.

"We wondered what happened—not like you, Greta. What's up?" Dax asked as he stepped out of the kitchette into the living area of his dwelling.

"Well, it's a long story...by the way, one of those wonderful 'neat' single—malt scotches would be very welcome just now—that is, if I haven't completely used up my welcome...

"No problem, coming right up, Greta," shouted Dax as he rushed back to the bar.

"Here you go," said Dax as he handed the refreshment to his guest, the shadow of a smile making its way across his tired and tanned face.

"Thanks! I really need this—I'll explain in a second. I promise, guys," replied Greta as she lustily guzzled every drop of the scotch.

"Okay, here it is. You both already know, and understand, I hope, that it is impossible for me to tell you where I'm going. All I can tell you is what you already know...that is, the plan has changed and the buyers have made other arrangements for the 'exchange' to take place. Evidently the 'buyer,' or buyers, got antsy, or maybe they're just being extra-cautious, but, in any event, they changed the game rules, and all I can tell you is that the location is out of the country. We don't know yet the precise location for the 'exchange' to take place. We're still working on that. But, no matter where it is, there's always a chance that there will be gun-play, or worse, once Interpol and the locals make the bust. Our quarry are master criminals, the killer-elite, the worst-of-the-worst. And, of course, Morgan, and Dax, we must do everything we can to assure that Laura is not harmed in this undertaking. As you both are aware, our info is that she is alive and, hopefully, well...our first concern is that she be rescued alive and well. Okay?"

Dax and Morgan said, as one, "Of course!"

Greta smiled, pointed at her empty glass, looked Dax in the eye, and asked, "May I have another? You do such a fantastic job on those 'neat' scotches."

"Your wish is my command, Greta. Be right back with a refill."

CHAPTER 51

Mikael knew now that this 'caper,' as his brainless boss called it, was going to be a bigger payday than any he'd ever envisioned. Bigger than any of the misfits he worked with could imagine. Mikael was a student of European History. Hell, he knew more than the 'king-pins' of the outfit. Most of all, Mikael was a student of the enigma known as the Amber Room. This enigma was a lost treasure of almost 100,000 pieces of multicolored amber, which had been intricately placed over three walls in the fabled Amber Room, a prime attraction in St. Petersburg, Russia, completed in 1756. The palace was a gift from the King of Prussia to Germany in 1716. Amber and gold had been installed by 70 artisans after the palace was finished. It boasted a 1,000 foot-long turquoise and white façade, decorated with 200 pounds of gold leaf relief, housing 52 chambers and rooms. The amber panels were framed in gold leaf, small mirrors and delicate figurines, giving the room the aura of a sparkling, magical music box. Two centuries ago the amber was lighted by hundreds of candles, aglow in fairy-tale glory...

Because the Germans were losing the war in 1944, the Nazi Command ordered the Amber Room to be dismantled and shipped in crates to the Konigsberg Castle in East Prussia, which is now the Russian exclave of Kaliningrad. Only problem was, the amber and gold disappeared. It was thought that perhaps the treasure had gone down in a German Ship, or was hidden elsewhere—at a location, or locations, unknown. Mikael knew that the world-wide search continues to this day; however, he also knew something his pals do <u>not</u> know—there was at least one crate of amber that was 'hijacked' by a Nazi Officer, whose name was never known, or revealed, to the world at large. And, that one carton had ended up in Mexico—the exact site was unknown; however, it had been reported over the years that it was hidden in a mountainous area, supposedly guarded by 'the devil himself,' or so the mountain folk in Mexico believed. It was reportedly seen at an re-enactment of an old Aztec tradition, or rather, Aztec event, known as 'Dancing with the Devil,' and tradition was that, if you danced with the devil, and survived to tell about it, you were entitled to see the carton of pure golden amber. Of course, the caveat was that you must never reveal the location. The penalty for doing so would be met by punishment by death—and a not particularly pleasant death...again, according to ancient Aztec custom, the culprit's heart, while still beating, would be plucked out of the perpertrator's chest...a 'medicine man,' one whom was aligned with both the Aztec God and the 'devil himself,' would do the honors.

    Mikael felt that this last bit of nonsense was just that—nonsense; yet, his belief in the existence of the fabled crate of stolen amber was real, and it permeated his thoughts, his existence...his life was dedicated to finding this 'pot of gold.' In Mikael's mind, this treasure of amber and gold was heaven sent.

    Mikael couldn't wait for their trip from Verdee, France, to Mexico. He knew that his bosses with the Russian mafia were intent on making the sale of the stolen art to the buyers, the Batista Family, who had made the call for a change of venue from Vendee, France, to Mexico. And, he knew they had no interest in pursuing this fabled lost treasure—this quest was to be his, and his alone, no one else invited to the party. He knew what he had to do—he would have to play his role, like he had always done...only this time, when he views that pristine carton of golden amber...well, he wasn't going to be in the mood to share any of it.

Mikael knew that his superiors would expect him to bring the treasure back to them—ha! They can all go straight to hell. He'd have the last laugh—he'd be kicking back somewhere on a tropical island, thousands of miles from the maddening crowd—at least, far from the Russian Mafia...he just knew it—it was his destiny, and he wasn't going to be denied...

CHAPTER 52

Greta Hammett knew that in the battle against cybercrime, identity theft, and terrorism, Interpol had a lot of company in the form of the governments of the USA, Canada, Great Britain, and the Middle East, among other smaller countries. She also knew that, when a U.S. passport is electronically read at an airport, it is important to have an embedded encryption in order to prevent problems with immigration officials. Her fave, and the fave of Interpol in general, is a digital signature input into the chip or magnetic strip. When this is done, it is absolutely tamper-proof. She also was aware that passports in at least six European countries and Malaysia have added biometric photos and finger-prints to foil counterfeiters. She recalled that Saudi Arabia, Qatar, and the United Arab Emirates all use encryption for their national identity cards, some with biometrics.

The main requirement is to have an all-in-one smart card developed so that Interpol's law enforcers, like Greta, can move, like a shadow, securely and safely, from one country to the next, and get inside any of its worldwide facilities in order to hook up at 'less than secure' sites. The cards look like credit cards to the casual observer, but they are critical in carrying out the duties of an Interpol Agent.

The only problem for Greta was that now, when she needed it the most, she couldn't find her 'smart' card. She didn't want to go through the hassle of getting a replacement, although that could be done, but that was a hassle she didn't need. She knew that if anyone, other than her, tried to use her smart card, Interpol would know it was an imposter, and would not allow clearance. However, that didn't alleviate the fact that she needed her card for the flight to Mexico, and that flight would be coming up tomorrow, or the day after, at the very latest.

CHAPTER 53

Morgan was worried. Again. But then, she was always worried—most of all, the concern was about her birth-mother, Laura. Coupled with worry about her mom in Helsinki—the woman who had raised Morgan from infancy, from the time Victor Vallinsky had decided that Laura would not raise Morgan. She understood the reasons for that decision, even though, as a youngster, growing up in Helsinki, she was troubled by the fact that she didn't remember her mother, had rarely seen Laura, from the time she was born...

Now that she was nearly nineteen, masquerading as a college student, she was on a quest, along with Dax and Greta, to find, and rescue, her birth mother, Laura Vallinsky.

And, now that she had so much on her mind, she was being thrust out of the picture by Greta, the Interpol Policewoman. Well, she understood, to some extent, why she and Dax were not going to be allowed to join Greta on the dangerous mission. She was sick over the inability to do anything at all. So, she had a plan. She'd have to talk it over with Dax tonight, get his take on the plan, and hope that he will be in agreement that it could work. She and Dax needed to be 'in the picture,' when the 'exchange' takes place, wherever it might be...

CHAPTER 54

The persistent ringing of his cell woke Dax from a deep sleep—the best rest he'd had since Laura's disappearance months ago. "Hello," he barked as he hit the floor.

"Dax, this is Greta. Can you meet me in an hour at the BLUE MATRIX? It's important that we talk before Juan Carlos and I take off on our trip. Okay?"

"You got it—I'll be there. See you soon."

ONE HOUR LATER—BLUE MATRIX ART HOUSE

Dax slid off his Victory motorcycle, locked the bike, pocketed the key, and walked briskly into the Blue Matrix. "Hello, he shouted, as he looked around and saw no sign of life...seconds later, Juan Carlos burst into the show-room and shouted, "We're in the back, Dax. C'mon in."

"Sure thing. Where's Greta?"

"Inside—come on in—we're short on time—okay?"

"You got it—got here as quick as I could—Greta said one hour..."

"No sweat—hey, you're on time—it's just that we're almost out of time before we have to shove off. They're sending a charter for us—will be in here in about thirty minutes, and they'll be rarin' to go. Come on in—Greta wants to talk to you before we leave."

Before Dax can reply, Greta stuck her head out the door and yelled, 'Dax, thanks for coming on such short notice. C'mon in, sit a minute and let's talk."

Dax did as asked, removed his motorcycle helmet, crossed his legs and waited for Greta to begin.

"Here it is...I think Juan has already told you that we've got to leave quickly. Okay, let me say that, although you cannot know where we're going, please know that, once this is over, and once we've got Laura safe and sound, I'll give you immediate news—"

"What about Morgan? She's dying to find out about Laura?"

"Of course. We'll call Morgan as well. It's just best that you two stay put until we get back to you. Okay?"

"Well, got no choice, but, hey, good luck, and you know that Morgan and I wish you the best," Dax said, his voice now a deep baritone, much deeper than usual.

"Well," Greta said, her face contorted in a manufactured grin, "got delayed and that put us behind the eight ball... misplaced my I.D.—no problem, I found it just a while ago... if it hadn't showed up, it would have been a major problem, possibly would have pushed us back a few hours on our trip..."

"What happened to it?" asked Dax.

"Well, hell, I don't know, one minute it's not there, then an hour or two later, it's where it was supposed to be...don't understand what could have happened to it—"

Juan Carlos spoke loudly, "Doesn't matter at this point—we gotta go, Greta."

"I know," Greta replied, her voice breaking as she tried to console Dax. "We'll let you know something the minute we can do so—okay?"

"Sure thing—you two better go now," whispered Dax as he jumped up and headed for the door. "Good luck on your trip, guys and gals, ' shouted Dax as he whisked through the door into that magnificent southern California sunshine.

CHAPTER 55

Morgan was late. Dax had pulled up an email from the teen an hour earlier, informing him that she needed to talk to him—about something urgent. She'd gone on to state that it was very important that they get together tonight at the Tropicana West. Morgan said in her email that she knew Dax would be rehearsing that evening at the jazz club. He'd emailed her back immediately to meet him at seven p.m—the rehearsal would be over by then, and they could have dinner at the club.

Dax glanced for the umpteenth time at his watch and noted that it had been almost two hours since her email—he was beginning to get worried about Morgan. Just as he polished off a Rolling Rock long-neck beer, the front door of the Tropicana West flew open, and Morgan trotted into the club, waved a greeting in Dax's direction, and plopped down on a bar stool next to him.

"Hey, sweet thing—good thing you're legal age, or we'd have problems with the law—you know this is an 18 and over club…

"Yeah, so what else is new? Dax, I've got to talk to you…"

"Isn't that why we're here? To talk? Shoot, girl—what's up?"

Morgan pointed at a secluded spot off the dance floor—a corner booth for dining, and asked, "Can we move over there?"

Dax frowned, noticed the serious look in her eyes, and replied, "Sure thing, Morgan. Let's do it!" They moved in unison to the corner booth as Dax signaled for a waiter.

Dax started to say something, but thought better of it when he saw the dark scowl on the young lady's face. "Hey, what's up, sweet thing? Something wrong? Did I do something bad, or what?"

"No—nothing like that. This is heavy-duty, so hold on to your hat, Dax. I've got a scoop for you...do you want to know where Greta and her pal, Juan Carlos, are going to make the 'exchange,' as Greta calls it?"

"Of course. But, how do you know where they're going?" Dax asked, his voice tinged with a hoarseness he hadn't been aware of, until now.

"First, let me tell you where they're going, then I"ll tell you how I found out—okay?"

"Okay—let me have it," Dax replied.

"Malinalco, Mexico. Ever heard of it?"

"Nope, I haven't. Where the hell is it, and how did you find this out?"

"First things first. Okay, Malinanco is not too far from Mexico City. It's in the mountains. It's an ancient site occupied by the Aztecs centuries ago—before the Spanish Conquistadors invaded Mexico and wiped out the Aztec natives and culture. It's in a valley ringed by mountains—sounds beautiful, doesn't it?"

"Okay—yes, it sounds great. Now, how did you find this out?"

"Did Greta happen to mention to you that she had misplaced her Interpol I.D.?"

Dax frowned. "Yes, as a matter of fact, she did. But, you couldn't use it—<u>could</u> you? I mean, she said no one else could use it but her, and if they tried, Interpol would know that it was someone <u>other</u> than Greta, because it was encrypted to her, and to her alone. So—"

"Okay, Dax. You're right. I saw the card—I didn't say I used it. When I picked it up, I noticed the outline of some scribbling she had done while at her desk, and what I saw must have been part of a writing tablet that she used—I mean, I didn't see the page with the writing on it—what I saw was the page 'beneath' the one written on, so, curiosity got the best of me—I shaded in the slight imprints from the pen she used, and what I saw was...well, here, take a look at it yourself," she said as she handed Dax a piece of notebook paper.

Dax held it up to the light, squinted and could just make out the following, "Wednesday, ten a.m., Malinalco, Mexico." He dropped the paper onto the table, cast a long stare at Morgan, and began, "Well, that's something, but that doesn't mean that's where the 'exchange,' as you called it, will take place. Right?"

"Well, it doesn't spell it out, but my money says it's where the deal will take place. And, if that's correct, then I think that's where we'll find Laura. What do you say, Dax?"

Dax scratched his head, rubbed his two-day beard, and whispered, "You may have something there, Morgan. You just might."

Morgan stared at Dax, and said, "I already know what I think, Dax. What I need to know is just this—what do <u>you</u> think?" Morgan's face showed no emotion as she spoke.

Dax could see, behind the façade of a young teen girl, the steel determination of a young woman who knew what she planned to do. A woman who would let nothing stand in her way. "I think you're right—this must be the place. But, how the hell are we going to find them, even if they're in this town I've never heard of?" Dax asked, his voice tinged with an increasing hoarseness.

"Dax, I don't know, but the thing of it is, if we're going to be there, don't we need to get out butts in gear?"

"Do you want me to make our flight reservation for Malinalco, or do you want the honors?" asked Dax.

"They don't fly from San Diego directly to Malinalco—we'll have to fly to Mexico City, then get a rental to Malinanlco—okay?"

"I'll make them for first thing tomorrow morning—okay by you?" Dax asked, his frown supplanted by the beginnings of a smile—the first one in a long, long while...

CHAPTER 56

Mikael and Laura walked down the steps from the private charter Mitsubishi air-craft and stepped onto the tarmac of the non-descript air-strip just miles from their destination, Malinalco, Mexico.

Laura still doesn't understand the role she is supposed to play in this wicked game—not only that, she hasn't been furnished a script. All she has been told was the terse remark from Mikael the day before, just as they left Challans, France, for Mexico. Her mind re-played a recording of that conversation, and it went something like this:

"Okay, Miss Laura, here's the plan—I'm going to go over this with you one time, and one time only—got it?" Mikael did not wait for a response—he continued..."We've had a change in plans—in lieu of making the 'sale' in France, we've found new buyers—with more money, and we've switched the venue to a little place called Malinalco, Mexico. It's really quite scenic, a small town nestled on all sides by mountains. I think you're really going to like it—that is, if you do <u>exactly</u> as I say. Got that?"

Laura nodded her understanding, Mikael continued... "I'm sure you're wondering what role you are to play in our little charade...don't worry your pretty little head—here's all you have to do: When the 'buyers,' arrive at the designated meeting place for the viewing of the art works, and make payment to, shall we say, 'the outfit,' in the agreed amount of almost $500 Million U.S. Dollars, then at that time you will be free to go...well, not <u>exactly free to go</u>—there is a caveat to the scenario—would you like to know what that 'caveat' is, my dear Laura?"

"Of course. You're going to tell me, whether I want to hear or not, isn't that the way it is?"

"I wouldn't have put it in that particular vernacular, but, yes, you are correct, Laura. You really have no choice, no choice at all. Okay, here it is—the caveat, or condition, I am speaking of requires that you be, if you will, part of the sale merchandise—that is, you go with the masterpiece art works, because, my dear, you are a piece of art, are you not?"

Laura's face was scarlet. "I'm not a piece of cargo—I'm a person—doesn't that mean anything to you—and your so-called 'business associates?"

"Of course, it does, my dear; however, the buyers have 'expanded' their business enterprise to include a very lucrative commerce known, in some circles, by the rather un-attractive name of 'human trafficking.' Personally, I don't like that particular term—rather offensive, I must say. I prefer to think of it as something akin to the Japanese 'old-school' term for a female companion, something like 'Geisha.' Don't you think that sounds a little more 'civilized'?"

"You can call it what you like—it's still slavery. Do you really think you'll get away with it?"

"Well, we've had you under wraps for what, seven months or more, is that right? Well, actually, it's more like seven and one-half months, and no one has come to your rescue...or have I missed something?"

Laura had no reply to that comment and decided at that moment that she would have nothing more to say to Mikael, or any of the rogues that posed as respectable 'businessmen.'

CHAPTER 57

Greta and Juan Carlos arrived in Mexico City, Mexico, just before dawn. Their initial destination was Taxco, Mexico, not far from their ultimate destination, Malinalco. And, they didn't want to arouse suspicion from the locals by appearing in town only twenty-four hours before the day the 'exchange' was to take place in Malinalco. At least, that was the latest information they'd been able to acquire through the auspices of the local and international offices of Interpol. They were planning to meet with the Mexico City Interpol Inspector working the case, Humbert Octavio. Inspector Octavio's instructions were to meet with Greta and Juan at the Santa Maria Hotel in Taxco. Octavio had explained to Greta and Juan that they could take a back road from Taxco to Malinanco which passes by the beautiful Hacienda San Gabriel de Las Palmas, as well as the scenic caves of Cachuamilpa, plus near the spectacular archaeological site of Xochicalco. This would ensure that their arrival in Malinanco hopefully will not be observed by the criminals they were planning to bust when the 'exchange' took place.

Inspector Octavio also explained to Greta and Juan that just a few months earlier, a mass grave had been found in a cave near Taxco, containing the bodies of almost seventy bodies, some mummified, some decapitated...the bodies been been 'dumped' into the abyss, almost fifty stories deep under-ground. It was assumed by the locals that the drug cartels were responsible for the killings and mass burials. Octavio told his fellow Interpol Officers, Greta and Juan, that he was glad for the opportunity to turn his attention, albeit temporarily, from the drug cartels to the business at hand, busting international criminals engaged in masterpiece art works theft.

CHAPTER 58

Dax and Morgan arrived in Mexico City by commercial carrier, thus avoiding the possibility of accidentally running into Greta and Juan Carlos. Dax had decided before they left San Diego that it would be best to stay 'out of sight' until such time as the 'business of selling stolen art masterpieces' was to take place. But, the burning question was, 'how in the hell do we accomplish that goal while at the same time we're trying to 'hook-up' with Greta and Juan'?

The only possible answer that Dax could come up with was the logical one, i.e., call Greta on her cell and let her know that both Dax and Morgan were 'in country' and on their way to Malinalco. He knew she would be pissed, but they really had no other option—he was a stranger in a strange land, and he knew he was out of his league, attempting to deal with master criminals and criminal 'buyers' of stolen art. He hoped that Greta would understand, and forgive both he and Morgan their reckless disregard of orders to stay in San Diego. His love for Laura, and, of course, Morgan's love for her birth mother was too compelling, too strong, for the duo to simply 'play it safe and stay put.'

So, Dax did what he had to do—he called Greta on her cell.

"Greta! This is Dax."

"What? Where are you calling from, Dax?"

"Don't get mad. I'm in Mexico City—

"How the hell did you know where I am?"

"It's a long story, but the fact is, not only am I here, but Morgan is with me as well..."

"Do you want to get yourself killed, and, while you're at it, get Morgan killed, as well? This is no Boy Scout outing we're talking about—don't you know that? Hell, Dax, this is not cool—not cool at all..."

"I know. I know—it sucks, but Morgan accidentally learned your destination—

"How did she manage that? I never told her a thing?"

"She saw a note on which you had scribbled the name of Malinalco, Mexico, and she shaded the imprint with a pencil to make it readable...she is one smart young lady, as you already know..."

"Too smart for her own good...you should not have come here, either of you..."

"Well, we're here, and want to help. What can we do?"

Greata's voice softened, almost imperceptibly, "Dax, you've got to keep your distance in this operation—it could be a life or death scenario—"

"I know. Just tell me what we can do that could help you out—anything at all..."

"Well, let me think—for now, stay put in Mexico City—when I give you the green light—*if* I give you the green light to proceed to Malinalco, I'll give you a call on your cell—okay?"

"Got it. We'll stay put 'til you give the word. One last question: is the 'exchange' on for tomorrow?"

"Yes, at noon. High noon," that's all I can tell you for now, Dax, other than be careful, be very careful..."

CHAPTER 59

Mikael was in a fine mood—in less than twenty-four hours, he'd have his share of the $500 Million to be paid for the sale of the stolen art he and his cronies had accumulated over the past twenty-five years—with the help, of course, of the tentacles of the Russian mafia and its affiliates, so to speak...

And, once he has his customary cut of the sale, which in this case, the biggest heist of his career, will be in the neighborhood of almost $60 Million U.S. Dollars, he'll have the money in hand to complete his endgame. And, this endgame would be the culmination of all his warped dreams, but, it would not erase the memories of a life-time, memories of being told that he was a loser, a first-class son-of-a-bitch, second to none. He had always been told, first by his mother, then his step-father, that he was a loser...

When you're told those things by none other than your loving parents, you have a lot of anger. Hell, you can't wait to get your revenge from those lucky bastards who had it made—had it made all their life, while poor Mikael had to panhandle, live on the grift, just to get by...while the 'upper-crust' had everything handed to them on a silver-platter... it wasn't fair, by God. And, he'd make them pay...hell, he had made them pay, hadn't he? Sure he had—over and over, again and again...this bitch Laura, who thought she was better than him, thought she was one of the 'upper-crust,' well, hell, he'd show her—he'd show 'em all—prove to them that he was not only a winner, but he would have a bigger 'roll' of cash in his back pocket than most of those miserable sons-a-bitches had ever seen...

Mikael shook off the bad thoughts that had temporarily raced through his head—he knew that he had to be at the top of his game, now that the stakes were so high...now, when it was <u>so</u> important that he play it just right, play it by the book, and not screw up...

CHAPTER 60

Greta and Juan had good news—the Mexico City Interpol Agents, working hand-in-hand with both the Federal and local Policia
In and around Mexico City had located a 'snitch'—someone who was known in the Mexico City vicinity as a person who works 'both sides of the fence,' so to speak... and that someone they found is none other than Miguel Calliente, a forty-year-old grifter. That is, someone who works as an informer when it suits him, and works as a crook when it is monetarily beneficial...of course, sometimes, bad things happen to those who choose to work both sides of the street, and the lesson that Miguel never learned, is just this: when you choose to walk on the wild side, sometimes you find yourself running down a one-way street...

Interpol had interviewed Miguel for the past eighteen hours, with only temporary breaks in the action for coffee and/or rest room trips. And, for the first seventeen hours, Miguel had stood up to the pressure. However, on the eighteenth hour, he shrugged, coughed up phlem from the pack of cigarettes he'd smoked since they brought him in for his 'interview.'

Miguel looked at his interrogators, both thirty-year policia men, and barked, "Okay. I'll tell you what you want to know. It'll cost me my life, if I'm lucky—if I'm not so lucky, it'll cost me more than that—I'll leave it to your imagination what that might be...

"Spill the beans, Miguel. Where is this 'meeting' taking place?"

"The address I don't know; however, it's on the road to Taxco, only about ten minutes from Malinalco...not far at all...it's a brown stucco, Spanish-style one-story house... think the owner is away on vacation...don't tell anyone where you got this information, or I'm a dead man—okay?"

"You got it, Miguel. Thanks for the info...you can stay the night, on us, in jail, courtesy of the citizens of Mexico City... meals are free. Lock him up, Hosea...by the way, Miguel, if this story holds up, we'll let you out when we get back, and I'll even buy you dinner—how's that for police cooperation? The Interpol Inspector laughed at his own joke and waved to the jailer to escort Miguel to his cell.

CHAPTER 61

Jaime Cepeda, the lead Interpol Officer conducting the successful 'interrogation' of the snitch, Miguel, put in a call to Greta Hammett. "Hello, Greta?"

"Yes, Jaime—you got something for us?"

"Yes, indeed. Okay, I'll give you a location, word-for-word from our informant, Miguel. Only thing I don't have is an address, but you won't need one—it's a brown stucco, Spanish-style one-story home, it's just about a ten-minute drive from Malinalco, on the Taxco Road leading to Malinalco...got it? Oh, almost forgot—the owners are out of town, so there's no danger of any innocent party getting caught in a cross-fire, in the event gun-play erupts when we make the collar...what time did you say the 'exchange' is scheduled to take place?"

"High Noon, straight-up twelve o'clock. And, let's see, it's already nine a.m., so we better get our act together, sooner than later. Can you be here soon?" asked Greta.

"Of course, I'll be there with about four or five policia. Why don't we hook up in Malinalco at the La Quinta Hotel, say, around eleven a.m. Okay by you?"

"We'll be there—thanks for the good work with Miguel—see you at eleven. Bye!"

CHAPTER 62

Mikael and his goons, three underlings he thought of as the Three Stooges, named Bruno, Mingo, and Karl, were early. Mikael had been instructed from the big boss in Berlin, Igor Stassi, to meet the buyers at exactly the noon hour, not a minute earlier, not a minute later—Igor wanted the transaction to run like a military operation, an operation in which every minute counted, and, unless there was a major problem which would need Igor's intervention, to have the operation concluded no later than one hour later, precisely at one pm, local time. So, since they had a little more than thirty minutes before High Noon, Mikael told his guys to 'kick back,' until they were approximately ten minutes from the 'magic hour' of noon.

Of course, these buffoons, none of whom had a grasp of the importance of timing, thought it was 'stupid' to wait, and Mingo, the brightest of the trio, with an I.Q. nearing seventy-five, spoke up, "Mikael, this sucks—why don't we head over there now? Hell, better to be early than tardy... right?" Mingo lost his moronic grin when he saw the anger flare on Mikael's face, and began again, "Well, hell, it's just an idea—have it your way—we'll wait, what the hell? I don't give a damn—it's your party—we'll do it your way, Mikael. No problem."

"I'm glad you see it that way, Mingo. Real glad. Now, give me a cigarette and shut up." Mikael said, as the onset of a smirk flitted across his angular face.

THIRTY MINUTES LATER

"Okay, boys, let's go—is the 'package' ready to go? I mean, all the art works have been sealed in the protective bubble-wrap for days, so they should be good-to-go. Correct, guys?"

The Three Stooges replied as one, "We're cool. Let's do it!"

Mikael glanced one last time at his wrist-watch, nodded back to his guys, and gave the command, "Let's go."

Mikael saw the two black Cadillac DeVilles parked behind the house as their Toyota Land Cruiser turned into the drive of the Burkholder home. Mikael knew that wasn't the real name of the owners of the home, but a dummy corporation had prepared the papers to reflect a Mitchell Burkholder as the owner of the home. Mikael didn't know, or care, who the hell this Burkholder character is, and, in fact, didn't know whether there really was a Burkholder, or whether this was a 'non-de-plume' for one of the upper-crust mafia commanders back in Mother Russia...it didn't matter to him—that was the set-up, and he'd play it by the book, like he had always done...this was, in some way, just one more job, but, on the other hand, it was not just any other job—this was the operation that would enable him to, number one, become a very rich man, and, more importantly, this job would allow Mikeal to realize a life-long dream, a quest he had been on since a young boy on the streets of no return, drifting like a piece of drift-wood...

If all went according to plan, once he had his share of the sale in his back pocket, he'd have more than enough finances to 'acquire' the key to all his dreams, achieve what he'd always dreamed of, akin to finding that pot of gold at the end of the rainbow, or bask in glory, like the protagonist of the novel and film, GUNGA DIN, climbing the Temple of Gold in a lost cause, lost but awash in glory—his memory and name forever framed in the blinding light of that wondrous, golden glow of The Temple of Gold...

Mikael shook his head in an attempt to focus on the business at hand. "Everything's good-to-go, Mikael," barked Mingo as he dropped on a sofa in the living room, as the foursome awaited the arrival of their 'guests.'

CHAPTER 63

Dax heard the blast of his cell phone and rushed to retrieve it before the caller could dis-connect. He and Morgan had already arrived in Malinalco, dis-obeying Greta's instructions to stay in Mexico City until she gave the green light to proceed elsewhere. "Hello, this is Dax!" he shouted into the cell.

"Dax, this is Greta. Where are you?"

"Well, I wish I could lie and say we're still in Mexico City, but I won't do that—hey, we're in Malinalco—I know, I know, you told us not to wander over this way, but I figured the 'action,' if that's the correct term, would be taking place somewhere near—

"That's precisely why I asked you to stay clear. But, since you and Morgan are already here, I'll tell you this, and <u>only</u> this...the 'exchange' is taking place at noon today...

"Noon? Hell, it's almost noon right now," Dax yelled into the cell as he studied his wrist-watch.

"Dax, you know you don't need to be anywhere near the location—it's going to be dangerous—we're dealing with very dangerous personnel, perhaps on both sides of the equation—I mean, I know the sellers are desperate criminals—not so sure about the buyers, since all we know is that, supposedly, the Batista Family in France are the purported buyers, but we'll have to wait and see when we get there, and, as a matter of fact, we're on the way right now. This could get dicey real quick, but we're doing everything we can to minimize gun-play, and hopefully, it'll go like clock-work, but, as you can imagine, you never know...

"So, what can Morgan and I do to help? Anything at all?"

"Stay where you are—that's all I ask—ok?"

"You got it, boss. Give us a call when you can—okay?"

"Will do. Gotta go—"

Dax put his cell on the desk in the hotel room and looked at Morgan—she had sat, Buddha-like, not moving a muscle, the only movement was a flicker in her eyes as she flashed her baby-blues in Dax's direction and pleaded, "What did she say, Dax?"

Dax relayed the message, word-for-word, then gritted his teeth and said, "I'm not gonna do it, but <u>you</u>, young lady, will obey her orders—that way, you'll be safe and sound—plus, you won't get thrown in the brig, or whatever the hell they do when you disobey Interpol...wait a second—you have to promise me you'll stay right here until I call you—okay?"

"You haven't told me what the hell you plan to do—you don't even know where the buy is supposed to take place..."

"Don't be too sure of that, Morgan, I have my ways of finding out what's up, but that's all I can tell you right now—time is not on our side—I've got to go...tell you what, stay in this room, and keep your cell close—I'll keep you up-dated on the goings-on...okay?"

CHAPTER 64

Dax had already noted two men—two men who looked like they were out-of-place, fish out-of-water...He knew it could be nothing, yet at breakfast they had consumed two pots of coffee, black, and had nothing to eat, other than two small apple desserts, south-of-the-border style...

Dax knew this, of itself, didn't mean a damn thing... but then again, these two, even in a town populated with tourists from all over the globe, stood out. It was no <u>one</u> thing; instead, it was a bevy of details, details that most folks wouldn't notice. But, maybe it was because of the gravity of the situation, or the stress he'd been under since Laura's disappearance, and, it was almost high noon—things were going to go one way—or the other—for the better, or for the worse, that question would be answered soon, <u>very</u> soon.

Dax grabbed his cell, bid adieu to Morgan and walked into the hotel restaurant. He did not see the two men who had been there for two hours earlier, so he approached the head-waiter and asked, "Hey, Garcon, have you seen my two friends who were here yesterday and this morning—drinking a tub full of black coffee?"

The waiter supressed a laugh, and replied, "Yes, two Frenchmen—they just left, about five minutes ago—"

"Did you see which way they went? I was supposed to meet them, guess I was a little late, and they couldn't wait..."

"All I know, senor, is that they took off in the direction of the Taxco Road..."

"Okay—got it—mucho thanks!"

Dax ran to his rental car, gunned the motor and headed down the road. He knew the car he was looking for was a black Lincoln Towncar and he'd find it if it killed him, and, deep in his heart-of-hearts, he knew it just might...

CHAPTER 65

Greta and Juan Carlos were watching from a vantage point about fifty yards from the Burkholder house—the host for the 'exchange' of nearly $500 Million U.S. Dollars for the purchase of priceless masterpieces of art...among them were works by Vermeer, Orozco, Rivera, Jackson Pollock, Willem de Kooning, Mark Rothko, Picasso, Californians Diebenkorn and John Marin, plus several other lesser known international artists of note.

They saw the four men get out of the Toyota Land Cruiser and enter the home approximately fifteen minutes earlier. Greta looked once more at the time—noted that it was just past noon—it takes two to tango, and only one group has showed...it's past noon, and she began to wonder whether the noon time-line was correct. Suddenly, a black Lincoln Towncar roared into view, and Greta and Juan were relieved that the game was about to get under way...

The entire area was being videotaped by Interpol and the State Militia Police cameras, out of view of the perps..."Let's give them a few minutes before we bust 'em," Greta said to the assembled troops via her cell phone. "Don't want to jump the gun and get ahead of ourselves. Once the money has traded hands and the art works have been delivered to the 'buyers,' then at that time we can take them down—everyone on board with that?"

Greta didn't wait for an acknowledgment of her question—it had been foreshadowed a dozen or more times already this morning—everyone was on board with the plan and it was 'game time.' Precisely at one p.m., the 'buyers' exited through the back door of the home, each man carrying a load of various sized packages—it took three trips for the three men to complete carrying all the packages to the vehicle which was equipped with a U-Haul type trailer for carrying the merchandise. But, Greta had to wait for the sellers to come out—the timing had to be just right, or there'd be utter chaos, and inevitably there would be gunplay, and this was what Greta and her companions wanted, if possible, to avoid.

Within seconds of the two men getting back into the Lincoln Towncar, three men exited the back door, and headed to a Toyota Cruiser. Greta gave the signal at that moment and uniformed officers converged on the site. Greta grabbed an electronic megaphone and yelled into the piece, "Everyone, hands up—this is Inspector Hammett, Interpol speaking—you are surrounded, drop your weapons and put your hands behind your backs—right now!"

In less than a heartbeat, all four hoods reached into their shoulder holsters, pointed 9mm Glocks in every direction. "Drop the weapons! Right now, or we'll be forced to use our weapons, and you better believe that you're out-gunned... okay, do it!"

Three of the desperados dropped onto the ground and began randomly firing in all directions. Mikael jumped into his vehicle and roared off in a cloud of dust, leaving his three comrades to continue shooting and take their chances. As it turned out, their chances were none too good...Mingo took a head shot and was dead before the policia could reach him, while his pal, Bruno ran, guns blazing, into a volley of rifle and small-arms fire—he was dead before he hit the ground. The third man attempted to run for it—he managed to get to the edge of a clearing just as a round tore through the back of his head...

Greta screamed for someone to follow the getaway car, but by the time anyone could get a vehicle started and on the road, the runaway, Mikael, was out of sight. "Okay, guys and gals—we'll have road-blocks set up—he'll never get to wherever the hell he thinks he's going," Greta shouted.

"Good idea, Greta," shouted Juan Carlos..."He won't get away. Meanwhile, let's round up the 'buyers' who are waiting for us inside the vehicle—too scared, I guess, to run...let's go!"

As Greta, Juan, and the Federales carefully approached the Lincoln Towncar, guns drawn, they were relieved to see both Frenchmen on their cell phones, hands raised in the traditional 'surrender,' signal...

CHAPTER 66

Dax could not believe what he had just witnessed...a full-scale shoot-out in broad daylight! And one of the shooters was trying to get away! The Toyota Land Cruiser nearly crashed into Dax's rental head-on. Dax had pulled to the shoulder of the road as he approached the Burkholder house on the Taxco road.

Dax spun the vehicle around, and gunned the motor in an attempt to follow the getaway vehicle. In less than a minute, he was pushing 100 miles per hour, and still, he was falling behind in the chase. Just when Dax thought he might be gaining on the Land Cruiser, his left rear tire exploded with an enormous roar—the rental vehicle went into a dangerous spin—Dax held onto the steering wheel, and hoped for the best as the car spun, ever so slowly, once, then twice, in a 360 degree circle...the car banked sharply to the right, whirled, topsy-turvy, through the air for a few seconds, finally coming to a rest only inches off the road. Dax thanked his guardian angel that he was still in one piece—he was amazed that his car had not flipped and burned. Dax managed to force the car door open, then staggered, bruised and bloody, out of the car. He wiped blood from his face as he gazed at the Policia vehicle racing toward him, sirens screaming as the car braked to a stop in front of him.

Two police officers, wearing black SWAT-style gear, guns drawn, approached Dax cautiously. "Hey, I'm Dax—a friend of Greta Hammett and Juan Carlos—they can verify who I am...I know I wasn't supposed to be here for this 'operation,' if you will—Inspector Hammett had ordered me not to be here...

"It's okay, senor. Ms Hammett had already warned us that you were in the area...she told us that you might, just might, <u>not</u> obey her orders and try to play 'cop for a day." Turns out she was right about you...

"Well, guess she was right on, at that. Say, is Laura there at the house? I mean, I had almost made it to the house where the caper was going down...I heard shots and saw the Toyota Land Cruiser hauling ass out of there..."

"Senor, how did you know the location of the 'caper,' as you called it?"

"I'll tell you anything you want to know, but I need to know if Laura is okay—is she at the house where the 'meeting,' took place?"

"There is no one in the house other than the three dead bodies lying on the grounds—we have taken two perp's—the buyers—into custody. There was no woman present...hey, let's get you cleaned up, then you can explain all this to Inspector Hammett...okay?"

Dax tried to smile, couldn't hold it, and replied as he spit blood onto the ground, "Sounds good—thanks!"

CHAPTER 67

Mikael was on top of the world. He felt like the James Cagney character, Cody Jarrett, in the 1949 Hollywood classic gangster flick WHITE HEAT, in which Cagney, portraying a psychopathic gangster with a mother complex, screamed at the police chasing him, 'Top of the world, mom...' although Cagney's character was dancing with the devil in a real death-waltz...

Mikael had pocketed, just hours earlier, his share of the sale, just over $60 million dollars, and his boss in Germany had been wired the balance of the money from the two Frenchmen, less the monies paid out to his three dead accomplices...oh well, those stooges had nothing to do with Mikael—he was king of the world, now that, number one, he had the $60 million, number two, he had managed to get away from the trap back at the house on the Taxco Road, although he didn't know how the hell Interpol had put it together...he also wondered how long it would take Interpol to shake down the two Frogs into spilling the beans about Laura. He knew they'd be forced to assist the Mexican Policia and Federales, as well as Interpol Officials, to rescue Laura, and save her from the fate planned for her in the human trafficking business...

Mikael didn't bear any real grudge toward Laura—oh, hell, he knew, of course, that she hated his guts—who could blame her? Certainly not Mikael. In a strange way, he felt good that she would be set free—that is, as long as her being free doesn't propel him into the long arms of the law. The hell with that kind of defeatist thinking. He was much smarter that the 'so-called' Mexican Federales and local Policia...and that goes for those over-rated Interpol bigshots. In any event, as long as he could stay out of their cross-hairs, he was 'home-free'...

Of course, the money was only a means to an end... what none of the stooges he worked with understood, including the big bosses back in Germany, was that Mikael had another agenda, and it didn't include being one of the 'boys,' for the Russian mafia, any longer. This dream was fueled by the legend of the missing amber from the fabled Amber Room—hi-jacked by the Nazis in 1944. Actually, there was only <u>one</u> crate of amber and gold...no one had believed Mikael when he talked about the missing amber— the stooges thought it was a fairy-tale—too wild to be true that millions, maybe even a billion, worth of amber was lying around, lost, all those years...

The difference between Mikael and his 'associates' was just this—he had imagination—imagination that propelled him to seek out, first, the facts; secondly, he possessed the drive to follow the leads relentlessly, until such time as you have either approved, or disproved, the theory in question. And, in regard to that certain missing carton of amber reported to be located somewhere in the mountains of Mexico, not far from Mexico City, he had determined, through scientific analysis and meticulous research, that in fact, this one carton exists, it <u>is</u> the real deal...and, the amber is located in the mountains surrounding Malinalco.

How does he know this? Because he had, unbeknownst to his superiors in Germany, made the trip to Mexico, just three months earlier. Mikael had used some of his 'vacation time' he had coming, and he wasn't going to miss his golden opportunity, just because he'd been baby-sitting Miss Laura

Vallinsky. He'd persuaded Mingo to take over his duties as watch-dog for Laura in his absence, on the occasion he travelled to Mexico City. Mikael had hired a guide to direct him to the clandestine source who had claimed to know the location of the one carton of missing amber. It was on this occasion that he was shown the carton of amber and gold, and its magnificance was indelibly imprinted in his brain. He had never seen such a glorious sight—it was as if he had glimpsed what heaven must look like...

The amber, even after two centuries, had glowed like nothing Mikael had ever seen—nothing he'd ever imagined. It was incredible—he knew, in the moment his eyes glimpsed the carton of amber for the first time, in his heart-of-hearts, that he'd never again see anything <u>remotely</u> as beautiful as that carton of amber.

CHAPTER 68

When Dax and the two Policia SWAT officers arrived back at the crime-scene on the Taxco Road, Greta Hammett and Juan Carlos rushed to the door to greet him.

"Dax!" shouted Greta as she grabbed him in a bear-hug, the beginnings of a smile trying to make its way across her face. She stepped back, cleared her throat, and began, "Well, looks like you couldn't leave well enough alone, Dax. You know your instructions were to stay away—you almost got yourself killed, and now...say, what the hell did happen to you? You look like you took a beating..."

"I saw one perp making a getaway, as I was approaching the house, so, I spun around and followed him—only problem was, I had a blow-out and crashed. Greta, these two officers," Dax said as he turned and faced the two men who had come to his rescue, and smiled. "They cleaned me up and brought me back to you. How's that for police work?"

"Well, I'm glad you're okay, but you should have listened to me—you could have been killed—

"I know. I can be really stupid. I'm sorry. Say, what have you learned about Laura? I mean, do you know where she is?"

"The two 'buyers,' French nationals, have clammed up—but don't worry, we know from our super-senstitive, top-of-the-line audio equipment we secretly installed last night, that Laura is in Mexico City—we just don't, at this time, know the location in which they have deposited her for 'safe keeping.' Don't worry, we'll get the information out of these two crooks—once they realize that we've taped their conversations inside the house with the Russians. That is evidence we'll use to convict them—and these charges will carry very long sentences. And, once they are charged with purchasing stolen art merchandise, not to mention, kidnapping with the intent of engaging in human trafficking... they'll give us what we want to know—no question about it. And, when they do talk, we'll find Laura and set her free..."

"Well, that's great, but how long do you think it will be before we get that critical information?" Dax was happy, although his escalating emotions simultaneously played hide and seek with his frazzled psyche.

Greta smiled and replied, "It won't be long. Trust me on that, Dax. We'll get the address, hopefully before the day is out. Once these 'not-so-wise' guys understand the ramifications of 'not cooperating with officials,' then, at that point there is no question they will be more than happy to give us what we want. And, when they do, we'll find Laura—I guarantee it. Okay? Feel better now?"

"Yes. But, until I see Laura—get to hold her in my arms, I'm going to be a basket-case," Dax said, his voice now a hoarse whisper.

"By the way, Dax, you haven't told me—just where is Morgan?"

CHAPTER 69

Mikael knew that the his career with the Russian mafia was at an end, and he was happy with the concept—he had known even before the 'bust' at the house on the Taxco road that this was going to be his last job. Now that he had the $60 Million in U.S. Dollars, he didn't need that life—he didn't want it any longer, and he knew that the 'arena,' as he thought of his circle of cutthroats in the Russian mafia, was no longer his—he knew he would be considered 'verboten,' bad luck. Therefore, he was 'expendable' in the vernacular of the 'family.'

His only interest, now that he had the funds, was to reach his contact—Humberto Fuentes, the same Veracruz native whom had led Mikael, only a few short months earlier, onto the trail of the missing carton of 2,000 year-old amber and gold...and, Mikael had seen the carton, in all its golden glory, and he'd have the last laugh, once he had paid for the carton of amber—hell, he knew it would cost him every dime of his pay-day—the $60 million would be his ticket to paradise—he'd be rich beyond his wildest dreams—why, the treasure could be worth more than $100 Million, thought Mikael. Even his lowest estimate of what he could expect to receive—would be more than the cash he had in his briefcase. Mikael knew it would not be safe to stay in Mexico City, or Malincalo, any longer—he'd already decided to camp out in the wild, until such time as he met with Humberto...

He knew it was only a matter of days, or hours, before he'd meet with Humberto. The problem was that he didn't know the location—Humberto was to contact him with instructions as to where to meet—he knew only that the location would be in the mountains. However, once the treasure was his, he'd transfer the crate of amber to a safe location...but, what the hell, he'd think about it tomorrow—right now he needed rest—it had been a long day...

CHAPTER 70

The jarring blast of his cell phone woke Mikael out of a deep sleep—he had been dreaming a recurring child-hood dream which had always played out the same way...

Mikael was nine years old, and he was alone—alone in a deep forest, surrounded by surreal, gigantic trees—the trunks of each tree as large in diameter as a circus tent in the Big Top. In fact, the forest was inhabited by circus performers. There were clowns, trapeze artists, and beautiful Arabian horses, all white in color. In his dream, he'd see the cotton candy and peanuts being hawked by the vendors, but he wasn't allowed to buy any of the treats. He would beg and beg, but it would do him no good...he'd try to protest to his parents, but when he turned to face them, there was only nothingness...suddenly, a ghostly apparition stared at him with the blackest eyes he'd ever seen...at that point, it always played out the same way—he'd run, screaming...only, when he ran outside the big top, trees in the dark forest would move toward him...The faster he tried to run, the faster the trees moved...he awoke screaming...what the hell was that noise? When the fog of the nightmare had finally relented, Mikael reached for his cell...

"Hello. Who's this?"

"This is Humberto. Are we still on?"

"Uh, yeah, of course. I'm sorry—I was asleep—bad deam. What time is it?"

"It's ten in the morning. Are you ready for our little trip?"

"You mean, today?" asked Mikael as he rubbed the sleep out of his eyes." I thought you couldn't meet for a couple more days—thought I'd camp out 'til then...

"Plans have changed—we need to do the deal today, or it's off," Humberto said.

"Just like that? Well, hell, let's do it—doesn't matter, today sounds good. Tell me where to meet you, and I'll be there," Mikael answered.

"Okay...that's more like it, compadre...

CHAPTER 71

Mikael was at the agreed location. Humberto had given him explicit directions to the meeting site—it was in the mountains near an area known by the locals as 'Hill of the Idols,' an old ceremonial site of the Aztecs, dating from around 1470...and being not far from the town of Toluca... the Aztecs used guardians at the gate, one of which was a depiction of an Eagle, and one a depiction of a Jaguar— these were the 'elite' of the elite Aztec warriors of the time.

He glanced at this watch, noted the time was almost eleven-thirty, just half an hour 'til midnight. Mikael wondered why Humberto had picked such a strange hour for their meeting. Well, he figured it must have something to do with the fact that at this time of night, they would not be as likely to have any 'unwelcome visitors' show up and ruin the party...

Suddenly, Humberto was beside Mikael, who had not even heard the man approach. "What? Oh, you scared me there, Humberto. I've been looking for you, but hadn't heard or seen a thing—

"That's because I didn't want you to see me. Don't worry. The object of your desire is already here. I had a couple of 'helpers,' if you will, to assist me in making the move away from the site where you first saw the wonder and magic of the amber and gold. These are trusted 'associates' of mine—there was no need, no need at all for you to meet them. And, of course, it's best that they not meet you. Correct?"

"You're right as rain, Humberto. Let's get on with it. No need to wait 'til midnight for the viewing, is there?"

"Well, actually, we do need to wait for midnight. Don't ask me to explain, just know that this is a fact, and a most important fact, at that."

"That seems a little strange, compadre. You never mentioned that before—

"Well, as they say in the funny papers, 'that was then, this is now.' Correct, senor?"

"It's your party. I've got the money with me for the sale—just like we agreed...$50 million U.S. Dollars..."

"Of course. No tricks, my friend," replied Humberto. Mikael stammered, "My 'former' pals, are no longer an issue—as a matter of fact, they were killed yesterday by the Federales...you might have heard something about it..."

"No, Mikael, can't say that I have, but, I'll certainly take your word for it, my friend. Let me call my two 'helpers' out of their hiding places to assist in your viewing of the 'goods.' Once you are satisfied that all is in order, we'll gladly take the $50 million at that time, and you can be on your way—of course, there is the matter of getting the carton of amber and gold down the mountain...did you say you wanted my men to help with moving the goods?"

"Yes, much too heavy a load for me to carry, alone."

Humberto didn't respond, then glanced at this wristwatch, noted that it was just minutes until the 'witching hour,' and said, "I think we can go ahead and get things underway. Are you ready for a second look into the most beautiful sight you'll ever live to see? I'm speaking, of course, of the carton of amber and gold..."

"I'm as ready as I'll ever be. Let's do it!"

Humberto raised both arms over his head and waved. Instantly, two men appeared, seemingly out of nowhere, as if it was all a dream. The night was pitch-black—Mikael thought that the men looked like apparitions...they moved in a snake-like manner, neither of the men seeming to move his feet—it was as if they 'floated' toward Mikael...

Once the two men were closer, Mikael saw that they were carrying the carton of precious cargo between them. They moved quickly, as if the weight were a matter of no consequence. In less than a minute, the chest of amber and gold was lying at the feet of Mikael. "Okay, Mikael, it's close to midnight, go ahead and open the carton," ordered Humberto.

Mikael didn't reply as he licked his lips and hungrily reached down and grasped the dual clasps holding the lid in place. With one mighty jerk of his arms, he raised the lid—the glitter of the contents temporarily blinded Mikael. He dropped onto his knees and rubbed his eyes—the light was so bright, it felt to Mikael as though the golden glow had burned his eye-balls. He recovered quickly, then thrust both hands into the riches that he had dreamed of—his dreams had been his retreat from the harsh reality of life in the real world. But, at this very moment, his childhood dreams had come true...

Humberto was not smiling. If Mikael had glanced at the face of his business 'partner,' he'd have seen something in Humberto's eyes, something that he would not like. Suddenly, Humberto motioned to his two 'assistants,' and in less than three seconds, both men had grabbed Mikael, stripped his 9mm Glock, and handed the weapon to their boss.

"What is this? Are you fucking with me, Humberto? We had a deal, you have the money, so, what's the problem?"
"The problem, senor, is most unfortunate—for you."
"What the hell are you talkin' about? We have a deal."
"Yes, and that is the problem, is it not? I mean, you are the stranger here, the 'foreigner,' if you will. And, please correct me, if I'm wrong, but, as you said yourself, your 'pals' are dead—they can't help you. In fact, <u>no</u> <u>one</u> can help you. Am I right?"

Mikael doesn't answer—he knew that he had taken a risk in dealing with Humberto without back-up...he knew, had always known, deep down—you always need back-up; even if it was in the form of those three dead idiots...where were they now? When he needed them most? Dead as door-nails, all three...

One of Humberto's 'helpers' clasped heavy-duty handcuffs onto Mikael's wrists, so tight that they nearly cut off circulation. Mikael tried to massage his wrists, couldn't do it, and aimed a look of pure fury at his captors. "Humberto, you are one scum-bag. What are you planning on doing with me now?"

Humberto looked again at his watch, noted that it was precisely midnight. He glanced toward Mikael and asked, "Are you familiar with any of the Aztec 'traditions?'"

"No. What about them?" spat Mikael, the venom in his mouth burned his tongue as he spoke.

"Well, tonight we're going to celebrate the season, being the 'Day of the Dead,' by a performance called 'The Devil Dance.' Ever heard of it?"

Mikael was in no mood for games, and he didn't like the sound of this 'game.' "Hell no, I've never heard of it—why should I?"

"Well, If you had studied up on Aztec mythology, you'd know what I'm talking about...it doesn't matter, the fact is, <u>you</u> are going to be the devil's partner in the dance...what do you think of that?"

"Go to hell—you and your two helpers!"

"Temper, temper, my friend. Remember, if not for me, you'd have never seen, what do you call it, 'THE TEMPLE OF GOLD,' is it?

"Screw you, Humberto. Screw all you bastards!"

Suddenly, the loud sound of beating drums assaulted Mikeal's ears; simultaneously, fire ignited the night sky. An 'apparition,' was it man, or creature, that whirled out of the shadows and into the fire...whoever, or <u>whatever</u> it was, something, or someone, carried 'fire' in its right hand. The apparition was painted, head-to-toe, with silver paint. His physique was that of an ancient God, and he was dressed like what Mikael imagined an ancient Aztec warrior might dress for a 'dance with the devil.' Mikael thought it must be the devil himself. The creature carried fire in his right hand— his hair-piece was bathed in all the colors of the rainbow. The 'devil' pranced up to Mikeal and taunted him, in an other-worldly voice, to 'dance with the devil.' Mikael didn't respond to the invitation, so the 'devil,' continued to gyrate around his prisoner, and taunted him, showering Mikael with ungodly names. Then the 'devil' lunged at Mikael and began to punch, and kick his victim, over and over again... all the while the 'devil' danced in circles, around and around his victim, an evil smile, rendolent through the war-paint and mascara splashed onto his malignant and fearsome face.

Finally, Mikael saw the shiny blade of a foot-long knife concealed in the right hand of the 'devil.' Before he had time to wonder whether the knife was intended for him, he felt the blade go deep into his black heart. Before he lost consciousness, he saw his life's blood draining out of his body. The last sight Mikael ever saw, just before he lost his battle for life, was the two 'assistants' placing containers to 'catch' his blood before it spilled onto the ground—his last thought before he lost consciousness was just this, 'hell, these guys are practicing 'blood sacrifice,' just as the ancient Aztecs of old...if Mikael had been able, he'd have laughed at the irony—blood sacrifice in the twenty-first century—who would believe it? Then, he tried to laugh, only no sound came out—mercifully, his life-force extinguished, the game was over for Mikael Pratt...he fell into a fetal position as he drew his last breath.

Humberto saw his assistants as they were caught up in the celebration of the 'cleansing,' then glanced one last time at the body of the unfortunate criminal known as Mikael, and said, his voice almost a whisper..."Men, you won't understand this, but as you know, I'm an instructor in the Classics at the university. And, the one thing I know about poor Mikael, is just this: he was so close to that symbolic, mythical 'pot of gold,' so close, he could taste it. Someone, long ago, should have explained to him—when he was still a young boy, that there is _no_ pot of gold at the end of the rainbow...yes, the amber and gold in the carton _is_ real—unfortunately, its reality set poor Mikael up for his ultimate fall from grace...

Mikael had told me that his favorite American fiction writer was named William Goldman, author of, among many other works, the novel, THE TEMPLE OF GOLD, in which the protagonist, the son of a classics professor, remembers what his childhood friend told him before his

friend committed suicide, and it went something like this...
"I know what you said, that there really is a Temple of Gold, but, I've got to tell you, there isn't any pot of gold...even old Gunga Din, was just a water boy, but he believed in that Temple of Gold...up until the moment he died—he didn't even have to be there—he was just the water boy...

"Well, the tragedy, or irony, if you will, is that Mikael didn't believe the story—he thought his pal was just depressed. In Mikael's heart-of-hearts, he wanted to prove there is a Temple of Gold. He believed that the trick is just this—if you just hold on to that belief, your precious dream—with all your heart, long enough, you couldn't fail to find that fabled pot of gold...it's a pity, poor Mikael had come so far, so far in pursuit of his dream...he must have felt in his soul that he couldn't miss—he believed in that pot of gold at the end of the rainbow—that was the driving force in his sad life, and, in the end, it had let him down..."

Of course, men and women will always look for that Temple of Gold—that mythic touchstone of the ages—they will look because they must...if they do not, they will turn in desperation to mythology's River of Forgetness, Lethe. The Gods of Oblivion are tricksters...the message is the same now as it's ever been...The Temple of Gold is inside of each of us, waiting to be discovered, time and time again, in each succeeding generation, and in each and every one of us...

"If only Mikael had been smart enough to realize that there was no way we could let him get away with the amber and gold, it was written in the wind, long before the stars fell from the sky, that the Gods will have the last laugh—listen, men, just listen to what the spirits are telling you—tread carefully, very carefully, when in the midst of something you don't understand...

CHAPTER 72

Morgan was excited—Greta had called and given her the news: Laura had been found by the Federales and Interpol officers based in Mexico City, and she was, thank God, alive and well in Mexico City. Greta had also told her that she and Dax would drop by to pick her up for the trip to Mexico City within the next two hours.

Morgan's anxiety of the past few days in Mexico, in addition to the 'waiting game,' in San Diego, had driven the teen to the brink of a nervous breakdown. She had rarely seen her mother from the time she had been spirited away to Helsinki to be reared as the daughter of the Fromme family, and she couldn't wait to see her mom again…

Dax knocked on the door of Morgan's hotel room, smiled at his two Interpol companions, Greta and Juan—the door flew open as Morgan let out a gigantic shriek of jubilation, "YEAAAAA! I can't believe it…I'm going to see Laura! YIPEEE! As you guys can see, I'm in heaven right now—absolute heaven!"

"Well, let's get your stuff loaded and we'll be on our way" Dax said as he grabbed the suitcase Morgan pushed toward him.

"That's it, Dax—the one and only bag I brought. But, if my memory serves me correctly, you have a couple, and I've already packed them for you—okay?"

"Hey, thanks, young lady. You are number one on the hit parade."

"What does that mean, Dax? A compliment or a dig...

"Whoa, guess I got ahead of myself there...I guess that cliché is more than a bit dated...you could say it's so old that its <u>way beyond</u> prime time...

"You're forgiven, next time, try to use language more 'in the moment,' so to speak, than a remnant from the 50s or 60s...okay, partner?"

Dax turned a whiter shade of pale, his embarrassment obvious to all, he swallowed hard, and whispered, "Thanks, Morgan—it is the twenty-first century, isn't it? I'll do better—cross my heart..."

Greta and Juan exploded in laughter at the 'scene' they'd just witnessed. Juan said, "C'mon, you guys, let's hit the road...Laura's waiting on us."

Let's do it," shouted Dax as he grabbed the bags and burst out the door, followed by his comrades-in-arms.

CHAPTER 73

Laura Vallinsky was worried. She knew now that the criminal low-life, the one who'd been her 'caretaker,' so to speak, the one whom kept her prisoner all those long, long months, since that eventful night in New Jersey when she'd been brutalized and then kidnapped out of the country… that low-life, Mikael Pratt, had somehow survived the shoot-out, while the three other thugs were shot to death at the crime scene. But, the thing that bothered Laura the most, the thing she still couldn't believe, is that the bastard of them all, Mikeal Pratt, had, seemingly, 'disappeared' into the night. Laura had been apprised of the situation, and she knew that there was no record of Mikael leaving the country. There had been no reported sightings of him anywhere in Mexico. The only visible evidence of his existence was the getaway vehicle in which he'd sped away from the crime-scene. A black 1988 Toyota Land Cruiser, fitting the description of the vehicle rented by a Ted Padesky, had been found by the Federales the day before. The Avis Rental sales person who had assisted this 'Ted Padesky' described the man as foreign-born, with a passport and I.D. indicating that he lived in Vienna, Austria. This was apparently an 'alias' Mikael was using in Mexico. And, the description related to the Federales by the rental-car person fit the description given to both Interpol and the Federales by Laura. The very man who had, over a period of seven months, beat and tortured Laura, both mentally and physically. She had been kidnapped all those months ago in New Jersey, then abducted out of the USA; first, to the heart of Russia, then to the Vendee area of France. Mikeal had referred to this action as a 'safe-keeping,' in lieu of the real name, 'kidnapping.'

However, the 'one' thing that had been uncovered in the search for Mikael Pratt was the getaway car. It was found at the base of a mountain, approximately one hundred miles from Mexico City. The vehicle had been wiped clean of any fingerprints, and there was nothing in the car, whatsoever. Curiously, it was parked just off the highway, near the entrance to a cavern. The local Policia and Federales had scoured the area, including the cavern, but had found nothing. It was as if the perpetrator of the crime two days ago had disappeared into thin air, or had never existed...

Of course, neither of these two alternatives were acceptable, so the search continued. There was no way the book would be closed on the case until such time as Mikael Pratt was found, dead or alive.

CHAPTER 74

INTERPOL HQS—MEXICO CITY

Laura had been pacing the floor, non-stop, for the past forty-five minutes, every passing nanosecond seemingly longer than the preceding one...she absolutely cannot contain herself much longer—the wait to see her lover, Dax, and her daughter, Morgan, has been too long...it's true, her captivity was behind her—but, she knew, in her heart-of-hearts, that the memories would never be erased—not in a hundred years. The pain of not knowing her fate, from day-to-day, minute-to-minute, had taken a toll on Laura, as it would have on anyone subjected to both mental and physical abuse; never knowing which day might be her last, never knowing what lay in store for her each time the key 'clicked' into the lock to the 'cell' in which she had been domiciled for those long, long months...

Laura hoped that the love she felt for Dax, and the love he may have felt for her, was not gone. She knew that it was possible that, although Dax had apparently stayed 'on the hunt,' for her, his feeling for her could have taken a hit in all that time...he could have found another woman...anything was possible...

Then there was the matter of Morgan—her only child who was not legally her child at all. Victor had made that decision—even before Morgan was born. Oh, she hadn't mentally accepted, at the time, that Morgan would be 'placed' with another family—a family far away from Berlin...

But, reality had finally seeped into her brain and into her inner-being, and, after many years of wrestling with it, she had finally come to terms with the fact that this was the way it had to be...she really had no choice—no choice whatsoever...

Suddenly, Laura heard the steps down the hall reverberating, more loudly as the steps got closer, then closer still to the office in which she had been pacing for over an hour. "Miss Vallinsky, you have company!" announced a voice from the hall. A mere three seconds later, the door flew open...

Laura stood still as a statue, her legs refused to move, although her brain shouted out instructions to her body to 'get a move on'...before she moved one step, Dax and Morgan were at her side, each of them wrapped their arms around Laura, the object of their mutual desire. "Laura! At last, at last," whispered Dax, his voice choking as he struggled to speak.

"Mother, I love you," cried Morgan as she cradled her mother, it was as if Morgan were the mother, and Laura, the child. Laura was speechless, her voice had gone off-duty, just as her legs had refused to obey her mental 'order' to move. Everything seemed to Laura to move in slo-mo, time had slowed to a crawl—she was in a magical space, a space where nothing was real, it's all in her mind...

Neither the Federales nor the Interpol officials said a thing. They just stood back and let it happen, reminiscent of the Paul McCartney and Beatles famous song urging the world at large to, "Let it be, let it be, whisper words of wisdom, let it be..."

CHAPTER 75

Only one day after the reunion between Laura, Dax, and Morgan, it was back to the business at hand. The three musketeers have been summoned for a three p.m. briefing by the highest ranking Interpol Officer in Mexico City, Raul Pizarro. Of course, the three top officers in the Federal Police Government, also known as Federales, being General Franco Aguirre, Colonel Nadel Esquivez, and Lieutenant Colonel Jacque Montenegro, were assembled for the briefing. General Aguirre slammed his wooden gavel down onto the parquet table top, and everyone braced to attention. The General coughed, then shook a couple of cough drops out of a bottle he had retrieved from his blue/green fatigues, onto the conference table. He cleared his throat, smiled a smile that was <u>not</u> a smile at all, and began to speak.

'Okay, if I have your attention, let's get on with it the meeting. Colonel Esquivez, would you be so kind as to 'enlighten' the assembled guests as to the latest news in regard to the international criminals who have attempted to use our country for their nefarious activity, which, as we all know, was the attempted sale of stolen masterpieces of art. The works are top-drawer, and all of the works we 're-possessed' so to speak, are, for the most part, of astronomical worth in today's art market. It's now common knowledge that these so-called 'master criminals' were intending to include, as part of the sale, Miss Laura

Vallinsky, whom they intended for use in the sex trade. 'Human trafficking' is the name for this most repugnant crime. It's scum that make a living by making 'slaves,' if you will, of these women, and, in many cases, children, some not even teen-agers. It's a crime against nature, a crime against humanity, and, by all that's holy, we will not tolerate it in Mexico City—by God, we won't tolerate it <u>anywhere</u> in our country. I think everyone present understands where we stand on this issue...correct?"

There was an avalanche of voices, rising as one, "We understand, General. No tolerance, none whatsoever."

"Good. Now to the matter of the 'mystery man,' also known as Mikael Pratt. A real 'piece of work,' that one. Yes, he <u>was</u> a piece of work, that is..."

"General—have we found him?" asked Colonel Montenegro.

"Well, the fact is, we've found what's <u>left</u> of him," the General said as he rubbed his gray beard with satisfaction.

Colonel Montenegro could not contain himself, and sputtered, "Well, General, personally, I hope he resides in hell for eternity, although that won't be long enough—

"A little patience, please, Colonel. As I was saying, evidently, our Mr. Pratt fell upon some bad fellows—fellows who still adhere to the ancient Aztec customs—most of which are re-enacted in various guises in night-clubs, and so forth, but there are some who must still practice the Aztec myths, or 'religion,' if you will; anyway, we found the 'body' of the unfortunate Mikael Pratt—the only problem was that his body was drained of blood. And, let me say, the corpse was in bad shape, as well—no need to get into this any further. We don't know who the perpetrators, are, but, in a large way, they have done us a favor...I'm sure there is a 'story behind the story,' but at this time, that's all I know. Any questions?"

The officers had no further questions, so Laura Vallinsky took advantage of the temporary silence, and asked, "General, excuse me, but now that we know Mikael Pratt is dead, does that mean the end of the investigation—"

"No, Miss Vallinsky. Of course not. We'll be working, internationally, with Interpol plus the various police organizations across the world, just as we always have. Any further questions? If not, we are adjourned," the General barked as he hammered his gavel once more onto the conference table.

CHAPTER 76

"So, Laura, how does it feel to be 'free' after over seven months of captivity?" asked Dax as he and his love huddled in their first opportunity to be alone. Laura had found a little bistro not far from the maddening crowd, far from the non-stop questions and interviews with first, Interpol, then more of the same from the Mexican Federales.

"Great—just great. And, Dax, let me say something before we go any further—okay?"

"Whatever you say, Laura." Dax answered as he swallowed heartily from his long-neck Corona beer.

"Well, the thing is, all the time I was held captive, not knowing, from day-to-day, whether I'd still be alive when the sun went down...well, the stress plays games with your mind. In spite of all the turmoil and privation, coupled with a little 'torture,' thrown in for good measure by Mikael and his buddies, I wondered whether I'd ever see you again...

Dax grabbed both of Laura's hands and squeezed them tightly, and broke in..."Laura, I had the same fears, actually, they were more like nightmares—or, as child psychologists call them, 'night terrors.' I don't think I realized, until you had disappeared, how much I love you—I love you from the bottom of my heart—

Laura leaned forward and planted a kiss on Dax's lips before he could continue...Dax didn't miss a beat as he wrapped his arms around the love of his life, and held the kiss for what seemed like mere seconds, but in fact the kiss lasted for almost two minutes—not long in a person's life-time, but Dax and Laura both knew that it was the kiss of a lifetime...

Dax knew that he was rushing the subject, but couldn't contain himself..."Laura, I know this is not the time or place, but I've got to say it—maybe, just maybe, when the time is right, and I know that time may not come for quite a while, but what I want to know is this—would you consider marrying me? Don't say anything just now...not just yet, but, when you're ready, I want you to know that I'll be asking you to marry me—whenever you say...besides, I don't even have a ring..."

"You silly goose...of course the time isn't right, but then again, timing isn't everything. However, you are correct that marriage is something we both need to consider once this 'chapter' of our lives has simmered a little. But, let me say this, and I'll shut up—I've never met anyone like you, Dax. If anything, my feelings about you are stronger than ever— let's give it a little more time, and, when the time is right, well..."

Laura's face was aglow with hope—hope for a new start, and the opportunity to begin 'anew' with Dax. And, maybe, just maybe, the chance to <u>really</u> know her daughter, Morgan. "Dax, once I'm cleared by the authorities to leave Mexico City, how would you like a little 'vacation,' so to speak, in San Miguel de Allende? It's not awfully far from Malinalco, and I hear that it's quite the 'artsy' place...sounds like it would be a good fit for us to visit—I mean, you and your love of cornets, and my love of the dance, well, it just might be what the doctor ordered for you and I to do a little kicking back—learn to enjoy ourselves, get to know each other again...what do you think? You up for it?"

"Am I? Hell, yes, I'm up for it. When do you think they'll give you the green light to leave Mexico City?"

"It won't be long, I'm sure of that. Of course, there's Morgan to consider—would it be out of the question to ask her to accompany us to San Miguel—I mean, if she wants to go?"

"No problem. I'm sure she'll want to go—might give you and Morgan a chance to 'catch up,' as well. Just don't overdo it—leave time for us to 're-acquaint,' as well...okay?"

"Of course, lover boy. Let's talk to her when we get back to the hotel,' Laura said as she finished off her Corona.

CHAPTER 77

SAN MIGUEL de ALLENDE

The next morning, the trio of Laura, Dax, and Morgan landed at the Aeropuerto Internacional de Queretaro Airport, located approximately forty miles, or seventy kilometers, from San Miguel de Allende. Dax had already arranged with the local transportation services to handle a ride into town, directly to the Casa Queyzal 'Boutique' Hotel, situated in the heart of San Miguel. He had taken a tip from Federale Colonel Montenegro, who had raved, on and on, about the beauty of the city and what a wonderful place to stay for first-time visitors to San Miguel. "It is absolutely unequalled, no question about it—at least not in my 'biased' opinion, senor Bolton. Don't even think twice—make your reservations at the Casa Queyzal—you won't be sorry—I can guarantee it."

Dax had made the reservations for one week—he knew that each of them needed to get back to San Diego. And, in the case of Morgan, she had to make plans for her return to the University in Montreal, and registration was only three weeks away. In any event, the threesome knew that they were in for the time of their lives for the next seven days... and, of course, re-focusing on the relationships of Dax and Laura, as well as the importance of Morgan and Laura getting to know and understand each other. It wouldn't happen overnight, but each one of the threesome knew that it would happen. For Laura, it was recovery from her captivity; and, for both her and Dax, the chance to re-ignite their romance. While Morgan didn't want to turn back the hands of time, she did want to live in the glow of her new-found life, a life full of the context of a mother/daughter relationship...

CHAPTER 78

Dax had made reservations for dinner and entertainment tonight, which was to be the last night of their one-week vacation in historic and beautiful San Miguel de Allende. He had anointed this trio 'The Wild Bunch.' They had made the most of their time together, and tonight was going to be the 'highlight' of their stay in San Miguel.

The reservation time was eight p.m. and the name of the night-club was 'El Toreador,' featuring exquisite cuisine, plus, according to the bell captain of their hotel, "the El Toreador has not only the best food in the city, on weekends it gets even better—they feature jazz on Saturday night only..."

"Did you say 'jazz,' my friend," Dax asked the bell captain.

"Yes, senor, jazz—some of what they call 'cool jazz,' and some of the more, shall we say, 'commercial jazz,' the kind you might hear on the radio, or television..."

"Well, hell, I play cornet in a jazz spot in San Diego, the Tropicana West. And, I played for almost ten years in New York, and my group, 'In a Mist,' played six nights a week—I was tired as hell most of the time, but the music kept me going—you know what I mean?"

"Well, senor, that's 'way cool.' But, unfortunately, I'm not much of a jazz connoisseur. But, there's no question you're going to like the El Toreador."

"Thanks for the recommendation—we'll be there tonight—you can make book on that, my friend," Dax said as he waltzed out of the lobby of the hotel.

One hour later, at exactly eight p.m, Dax and the other two members of the 'Wild Bunch,' that is, Laura and Morgan, arrived at the appointed time for dinner, drinks, and some 'cool jazz.' "Senor, Senoritas, this way, please follow me," smiled the garcon, whom had signaled to the wait-staff for a waiter to accompany the three customers.

One hour later, the 'Wild Bunch,' had taken full measure of their dinner. It was, in the waiter's words, "Heaven on earth—in the form of the best food you'll find anywhere in the universe—or, at least in San Miguel de Allende. He'd even pointed out a 'north of the border' celeb who'd apparently made a home in San Miguel, none other than John Davidson, singer of repute and a former 'stand-in guest' on the TONITE SHOW, subbing for none other than Johnny Carson.

But, the 'main course' of the evening, at least in the mind of Dax Bolton, was the entertainment—he couldn't wait to see if they had the 'chops' as advertised. The bell captain at the hotel had 'guaranteed,' that they were the 'best in the land.' In no time, the quintet took center stage and spent a few minutes 'tuning up' prior to the 9:30 p.m. start time.

At exactly five minutes past nine-thirty, the band, named 'Helter-Skelter,' cranked it up, and the music drifted in, seemingly floating above the customers, who were busily engaged in chatter, as well as consuming their 'libations' and food-stuffs, all of which looked, and smelled, delicious.

Dax eased off his third margarita, settled back into his chair, he was eager to see if these guys and gals had 'the goods,' to play his kind of music—cool jazz...it didn't take long before Dax was satisfied that he had been led to the right spot. The music was intense, while subtle at the same time...like the music Dax most favored, the jazz seemed to be a narrative of opposites...that is, the music was a study of light against the dark, or 'easy listening' brushing up against its dark cousin, dissonance against pure intervals of sound...Dax laughed to himself as he finally understood what his fans meant when they told him that his cornet sounded like a girl saying 'yes'...Dax recalled a review in THE NEW YORKER when he played in Brooklyn at the Blue Moon...he remembered every word..."Dax's horn is the template for 'micro-tonality,' in other words, the division of the octave into more than the usual twelve pitches that we normally associate with it...his music gives the listener a seemingly 'exalted,' if you will, glimpse of sound—a sound that lingers in the recesses of the mind..."

Dax shook his head in order to prevent himself from lingering too long over the review—he'd had his share of both good and bad—it just didn't pay to listen to your critics too often—if you put too much stock in what they said about you, it could put your head into a cloud, or dig you a path deeper into Hades that you'd ever want to go.

Suddenly, Dax sat on the edge of his chair as he recognized the piece the band had just started playing... it was none other than "Rhapsody of Blue,' a symphonic jazz-work, all the tunes encompassing songs either written or performed and popularized by none other than Dax's hero, Bix Beiderbecke. Dax was on the edge of his seat as the band stopped for a fifteen minute break...he didn't say a word to his two companions, Laura and Morgan, as he bolted out of his chair and approached the leader of the group.

"Hello. You don't know me, but I'm a horn player—cornet, that is. My name's Dax Bolton—I play at the TROPICANA WEST, in San Diego, California, and my former group, 'IN A MIST,' played for ten years before that in Brooklyn, New York, at a little place called the BLUE MOON...

"Well, hell, Dax, I didn't recognize you—I saw you play at your last gig in Brooklyn—what, five months or so, was it? Hell, it was my first trip to New York, and I had heard about you from some of my cronies, and they all said, 'be sure and check out the BLUE MOON in Brooklyn,' and they told me about your love of Bix. Shoot, that's my fave too, that's why we're playing—

Dax interrupted, and said, "You're playing one of my all-time favorites, 'Rhapsody for Bix,' I love it—just love it—"

"Well, Dax, would you like to join in—play a little cornet for us—

"I don't have my horn, or horns, with me—you may recall that I play the E(Flat) as well as B(Flat) horn—I have matching silver cornets, love those horns—they're my 'babies'...

"Well, just so happens I've got a couple extra—they're both B(Flat)—you'll have to get by with one of them...

"No problem. Yes, I'd love to play—take me to the horns and I'll limber up my lips—okay?"

"You got it—anything for Dax Bolton—hell, Dax, if you'd told me who you were, I'd have had them 'comp' you for the dinners and drinks...I can still talk to the wait-staff...

"Nah, thanks, but we'll pay our bill—just want to get up there with you and your guys and gals—love to play the cornet—that's what gets me up every morning...

"Ha! I know what you're talkin' about...follow me, Dax. I'll take you to the horns.

TEN MINUTES LATER

Laura and Morgan sat still as statutes as Dax walked back to their table and told them he'd be joining in with the band after the intermission break. Laura was shocked—"Dax, did he recognize you, or what? I saw you speaking to him and he looked at you as if you two were old pals...

"Would you believe that he caught our act on the last night I was in Brooklyn, the night before I left for San Diego—the night that Lulu Fontaine, of Paris, France, joined us, and I introduced a little number I'd just written, called 'A BLUE, BLUE HEART.' Lulu sang the lead, I sang chorus, and played those two cornets like they'd never been played...I still get notes from folks who heard us that night...by the way, Laura, Miss Morgan here has heard A BLUE, BLUE HEART, haven't you, Morgan?"

"Sure have, Dax. You also had Lulu for that performance. Right?"

"You're right as rain—it was totally un-expected, but I managed to line her up at the last minute...

Laura shook her head as her face turned from an incredulous look to a grin; finally, a full-fledged smile graced her face, and she finally managed to respond, "Well, Dax <u>really</u> is an international celeb...whaddya' know, Morgan? Well, Dax, its good you've warmed up—we don't want you looking bad, here in San Miguel...who knows, John Davidson might want to get up on the stage and sing for you..."

Dax laughed and said, "I don't see Mr. Davidson here any longer...oh, well, we'll have to do without him, I suppose... gotta go, girls—work calls..."

CHAPTER 79

 Dax waited for the girls to meet him at the check-out desk at the Casa Queyzal Hotel—it was just ten minutes to take-off time for their departure to the airport for the flight to San Diego. Last night, after a great time at the 'Helter-Skelter' night-club in San Miguel, Dax and Laura said 'good night,' to Morgan. Dax had escorted Laura to her room, and the memory of those fleeting hours rushed back into his mind…they made love as if their lives depended upon it…each one tried to make up for all the wasted time—the seven months that had been stolen from them…

 Dax caught sight of the girls walking toward him—they hadn't yet seen him—he was standing in the shadows, just out of their sight. He fixed his gaze on the love of his life, none other than Miss Laura Vallinsky. He had never understood what it was about the woman that so enraptured him, body and soul. Suddenly, a thought bolted through his mind, something that had not occurred to him previously…it was as if, within Laura's persona, there was 'something' deep inside of her that was impossible to categorize, impossible to put into words, but, this thought ran through his brain…it's as if Laura has a form of 'spiritual isolation,' something that could draw a person to her—even while Laura simultaneously was distancing herself from the unwanted attention. Is that even possible, he wondered? However, no matter what it was—or what it was not, the fact remained—he was deeply in love with her…her serene smile had reminded him on the day they met of what the Greeks call an 'archaic' smile—a smile so sublime that it doesn't appear to be a smile at all...

Dax would not rest, until such time as they were together, lovers 'til the end of time—and that's a long, long time...

FIN

ADDENDUM

A BLUE, BLUE HEART
THE LYRICS

BY

Dax Bolton
Copyright 2012

INSTRUMENTAL: CORNET, ELECTRIC BLUES GUITAR/KEYBOARD

LEAD VOCALS: We met at the Blue Moon...
    Our love began, and ended, much too soon...
    You wore white—I wore black,
    I need my baby back...

    Lost in a crazy dream,
    Trapped in a cosmic moonbeam,
    Can't believe you're no longer mine,
    Afraid it's all been wasted time

(CHORUS) You said we'd never part,
    I've been your fool from the start...
    How do I mend a blue, blue heart?

LEAD VOCALS: Why can't I forget your face?
    Be smart, end the race...
    I only know...miss you so...
    The memories just won't go

    Lover, please return to me,
    The Blue Moon beckons to melancholy lovers,
    We'll dance 'til the end of time,
    Lover, high-hatted lover, please be mine...

(CHORUS)You said we'd never part,
 Did we dance to the end of love?
 And how do I mend a blue, blue heart?

LEAD VOCALS:I'm not so smart,
 You're the only cure for my torn...(beat)
 Blue, blue, heart,
 Lost in a crazy dream,
 Trapped in a cosmic moonbeam,
 Can't believe you're no longer mine...
 Afraid it's all been wasted time...

 You said we'd never part,
 Did we dance to the end of love?
 How do I mend a blue, blue heart?

INSTRUMENTAL:CORNET SOLO (MUTED)

TAG:AT THE END OF LOVE,
 How do I mend a blue, blue heart?

PAUSE:

AT THE END OF LOVE,
 You're the only cure for my torn...(beat)
 Blue, blue heart...

REPEAT:
AT THE END OF LOVE,
 You're the only cure for my torn...(beat)
 Blue, Blue heart...

(REPEAT TAG TO FADE)

Would you like to see your manuscript become a book?

If you are interested in becoming a PublishAmerica author, please submit your manuscript for possible publication to us at:

acquisitions@publishamerica.com

You may also mail in your manuscript to:

**PublishAmerica
PO Box 151
Frederick, MD 21705**

We also offer free graphics for Children's Picture Books!

---

www.publishamerica.com

CPSIA information can be obtained at www.ICGtesting.com
Printed in the USA
LVOW051658081212

310645LV00001B/31/P

9 781462 695980